THE DOCTOR'S DAUGHTER

THE DOCTOR'S DAUGHTER

•

Amy Blizzard

AVALON BOOKS
NEW YORK

Bli

Published by Avalon Books,
an imprint of Thomas Bouregy & Co., Inc.
160 Madison Avenue, New York, NY 10016

Library of Congress Cataloging-in-Publication Data

Blizzard, Amy.
    The doctor's daughter / Amy Blizzard.
        p.   cm.
    ISBN 978-0-8034-7707-0 (acid-free paper)
    1. Physicians—Fiction.   I. Title.
    PS3602.L6D63 2010
    813'.6—dc22

                                2010022405

PRINTED IN THE UNITED STATES OF AMERICA
ON ACID-FREE PAPER
BY HADDON CRAFTSMEN, BLOOMSBURG, PENNSYLVANIA

For my mother, Kathleen Blizzard, and dear friend, Mare Forkin. Thank you for always believing in me and this story and for supplying endless encouragement.

My Willie, I will always love you.

Acknowledgments

Thank you to my beautiful grandmother, Marlett Hurt, for sharing her love, talent and creativity with me and planting the seed that blossomed into a passion for the creative arts.

Roy Hurt, my amazing grandfather, thank you for playing a part in my fondest memories and showing me love is expressed with much more than words.

My great-aunt, Bertha Louise Hurt, your warmth, unwavering support, and hugs are dearly missed.

P. Bear and Angel, I love you.

Leah, thank you for reading my stories, even when they were written in pink ink and glitter, and for believing I would be an author even when I didn't.

Mr. Atkins and Mrs. McNeely, thank you for inspiring your students to not let creativity fade away with childhood.

I would also like to express my gratitude to the following people for their love and support:

Aunts and uncles: Kelly, Kerry, Sherry, Ric, and Jason

Cousins: Heather, Will, Tony, Joy, Kristina, and Katlynn

Friends: Mary, Brandie, Kat, Stacey, and Angie

Chapter One

Ain't it beautiful here?" Pap Dickens boasted as his stagecoach drove past green fields and meadows covered with wildflowers of every color.

"It's primitive," Dr. John Carson complained under his breath while the stagecoach traveled along the bumpy hills of Missouri.

Since the unlikely pair had left the train station in Saint Louis, the young doctor had seen nothing but open fields and farms loaded with grazing animals. It was the complete opposite of the life he had known in Boston. Saint Louis had seemed promising; not as ravishing and modern as Boston, but a city nonetheless, with tall buildings and people crowding the streets. But the images of the city were now only a memory as the stagecoach traveled farther and farther away.

"I can't believe you don't have a train station in your town!" he bellowed to the eccentric, elderly driver seated beside him. "You'd think by 1886, they'd have a station in every town and city like they do in the East."

Pap chewed lazily on the piece of hay stuck between his

lips. "Ain't got much need for a train station in Templeton. Everybody knows everybody, and anytime a stranger like you comes in from yonder, why my stagecoach does right fine to bring 'em into town."

"Stagecoach," John mocked, rolling his eyes at the rickety old wagon that nearly fell over each time they went up a hill. "A proper stagecoach does not require a passenger to sit by the driver. And is that a *donkey* pulling this thing?"

"Lulu may not be a stallion, but the old girl has done good bringin' folks into town and gettin' folks around town," Pap praised, smiling at the gray donkey. "You don't need no big horse to do the job."

"Maybe not," John admitted, "but a proper place to put luggage would be nice! My bags were tossed into the back like they were bales of hay. There are breakables in there, mind you."

"I sure do hope you mean medicine bottles. There's a bad spread of sickness back home. That barlett fever took our dear Dr. Bethel, God rest his soul. Town couldn't ever asked for a better doctor than Gene Bethel."

"You mean *scarlet* fever," Dr. Carson corrected irritably. "And I'm sure I'll be able to handle whatever disaster your town is dealing with. Besides, from the way you describe it, there couldn't be more than ten people living there."

Pap burst out in laughter, causing the stray piece of hay to fall from his mouth. "Ha, did I make it sound that small? Well, Templeton is definitely a tiny place, but there's more than ten people. You're the talk of the town, young feller. Everybody's real excited to meet the new doc. Nobody ever seen a guy quite like you before."

John glanced at his own tailored blue suit and straightened his matching hat, then observed the driver's dirty, tattered overalls, unruly white beard, and large straw hat. "Shocking," he mumbled.

"If you don't mind my asking, Doc," Pap continued with

his relentless questions, "why'd a fancy guy like you accept a job to be a doctor out here?"

Good question, John thought to himself. Why had he abandoned his life in Boston to begin his practice in this rural jungle?

"Because I have nothing else, that's why," he confessed in a whisper.

"What was that? I didn't hear you, kid."

"It wasn't important. And why does it matter why I came?" Dr. Carson asked defensively. "Templeton is in dire need of a doctor and in the middle of a local outbreak. Now isn't the time to be picky. I intend to do my best to quickly end the problem and return your lives to normal—whatever that may be. But I would appreciate it if you could fill me in on the situation, Pap."

"Well, there's not too much to tell. As you mighta guessed, I ain't got much doctor knowledge. I just know the kids in town been awful sick and it's spreadin' like a bad rash. Some of the youngins even gave it to their folks. There's whole families sick. But I never thought that our Dr. Bethel would catch it and die. God rest his soul," Pap said once again, bowing his head.

John sighed and shut his eyes. It appeared that this small town had placed their old doctor on a pedestal that he could never reach. Opening his eyes, he looked back over his shoulder, wishing the train station that could lead him back to Boston would still be in view. But it was much too late. Even if this situation seemed to be doomed from the start, he had committed himself to help out the people of Templeton and he would do everything in his power to do so, despite the unpleasant circumstances.

"Besides Dr. Bethel, have there been any other fatalities, Pap?" the young physician inquired.

"Any what?"

"Deaths," John simplified, using all of his willpower to fight off a disparaging tone.

"Oh, only Dr. Bethel and the McGuivers' baby boy."

Dr. Carson nodded silently, thankful to learn only the life of an older man and young infant had been taken. Naturally, he would never be grateful to hear of the death of any patient, but he was relieved to learn only the most susceptible patients had succumbed to death and normally healthy adults and children had been able to fight off the illness.

"If the town is so badly stricken with scarlet fever as you mentioned, how on earth have you been so fortunate to only have one death besides the passing of your town doctor?" he questioned with genuine interest.

Pap pasted on a big grin. "It's all thanks to Sarah, Doc Bethel's daughter. She's been an angel for our town. Don't know how on earth we all woulda got by if it weren't for her. I don't know how she's doin' it all on her own after just losin' her pa."

"Why doesn't her mother help her? Is she too grief stricken?"

"Her ma died in childbirth. Her pa's all Sarah ever had, that's how come she knows so much. She's even the one that contacted her pa's college to find out if they could send anyone to come out and help us. Sarah's turned the schoolhouse into a hospital for everybody that's got the fever, and she's been treatin' them best she can. Mighty fine woman she growed up to be."

"Well, at least she had several years with her father before she was left all alone," John muttered.

"What?" Pap asked, straining to hear. "Sonny, you're gonna have to stop that whisperin' nonsense, or else nobody's ever gonna know what yer sayin'."

Then it will be mutual, John wanted to say, but instead replied, "I'm glad to know you have a nurse who can help me treat patients."

"She'll be a big help to you, Doc, just like she was to her pa. Don't you worry about that."

John tilted his hat against the bright sunlight that shone downward and heaved a sigh. Not only did Templeton, Missouri, worship Dr. Gene Bethel, but they loved his daughter too. As Pap chattered on and on, a part of John wondered if the town really needed his help. And why did the stage driver know so much? Back home in Boston, it wasn't unheard of to not know the name of your next-door neighbor, let alone their business.

"Welcome to Templeton!" Pap Dickens announced suddenly with pride, sticking out his scrawny chest.

John lifted his hat and looked over the grass-covered hills to what appeared to be the first sign of civilization he had seen after hours of staring at fields and meadows. Beyond the hill, a small cluster of buildings stood neatly side-by-side, looking like cabins when compared to the glorious architecture that layered the streets in Boston.

"So, what do ya think?" Pap asked curiously as the stagecoach made a bumpy turn onto the town's dirt roads and blew a gust of dusty dirt into the air.

"It's different." Dr. Carson coughed, removing a handkerchief from his pocket and covering his mouth. "That's for sure."

"Different can be a good thing."

John sighed as he took in the humble sights in the tiny town. Only one thing could make him thankful to reside in Templeton: the house he had been promised when he agreed to accept the job offer in Missouri. A beautiful home built by the townspeople as a thank-you to their old doctor, and he was ready to take the home as his thank-you for coming so far and leaving everything he had ever known behind.

For the first time in his life, he would have a home to call his own, a home that was truly his and his alone. Perhaps the country earth and the simple people who surrounded him would be a large adjustment, but his house would serve as a deserved sanctuary.

"Pap," John said, turning to the stage driver, "how much longer until we get to my house?"

"Your house?" Pap repeated slowly, turning quiet and shy for the first time all day.

"Yes, my house," he replied happily. "The one built for the doctor by your town's citizens. That house is practically the sole reason I accepted this job offer. Deals like this are rare in Boston, and I'll be glad to have some space of my own after residing in a cramped, lowly boardinghouse for nearly a year."

"There will be time to see your house, Doc, I'm sure. But I just . . . well . . . I figured you'd tend to the sick first."

John sighed and nodded his head. "Yes, I will. I guess I was letting my excitement get the better of me. Of course I will assess the condition of the ill townspeople first."

"Oh, Pap! Pap!" a high female voice called out suddenly, filled with the same accent as the elderly man. "Is that the new doc?" the older woman asked, and came hurrying out of one of the wooden buildings.

"Sure is, Betty," Pap answered, patting John's shoulder as he quickly returned to his old self. "I just got him from the train station, gonna take him straight to the sick folks. Sarah still at the schoolhouse with them?"

"Yes. And from what I hear, now the Rivers' youngins are there with mighty bad fevers."

John rolled his eyes; he wasn't sure what spread faster in Templeton: townspeople's business or scarlet fever.

"Eve and Samuel?" Pap replied sadly as his shoulders drooped. "What a pity, they're such good kids. But hopefully now that the doc is here, they'll be just fine. Betty, I want you to meet Dr. John Carson, all the way from Boston."

"Oh, I know who he is!" Betty chuckled, pushing back the sides of her blue bonnet to look up at him. "Whole town's been talking about him for days. Pleased to meet you, Doctor. I'm Betty North. I run the post office here."

"Nice meeting you, ma'am," Dr. Carson replied perfunctorily, though grateful to learn his new home at least had a postal system.

"I sure do hope you'll be able to put a stop to all this sickness," she rambled.

"Likewise," John responded, this time genuinely. "I'm sorry to go so quickly, but I do believe I must be getting over to the schoolhouse to see what I'm dealing with."

"No need for that sorry business. I understand. Pap, I know you've gotta help this new doctor get settled in, but you think you might be able to ride out to my place later?" Betty asked, her cheeks turning rosy. "I have a fence that needs mendin'. I could make you some supper to pay you for yer help."

"Oh, Betty, you know you never need to pay me. But supper'd be mighty nice, anyhow. I'll be over after I show John around."

"All right," Betty replied, simply beaming. "Well, I'll see you tonight, then. Good luck, Dr. Carson, and thank you so much for comin'." She reached out and took his hand. "God bless you."

"Thank you," he replied briskly, giving her hand a quick shake. "Good day, Mrs. North."

"Giddyap!" Pap called out to his donkey, tugging at the reins, and once again the wheels of the stagecoach were turning and leaving a dusty trail behind their path. "Schoolhouse is just up the road. You ready to start your job, Doc?"

The question rang in John's ears. Was he ready for this? For the past year, he had been treating patients at Saint Francis, one of the most highly respected hospitals in Massachusetts. There was barely any injury or illness he hadn't seen up close and treated. But even if he had been a star medical student under the tutelage of Dr. Thompson, had been trained inside foul orphanages, and later gained an impressive cure rate on his own merit, he had never been on his own to handle an epidemic. At the hospital, there were several other doctors just as talented and intelligent to help care for all the patients and handle the occasional outbreaks that swept through the city.

Shutting his brown eyes against the dust that blew up in the heavy breeze, the doctor's mind flooded with memories of the cold, drafty rooms filled with sick children who had been long forgotten inside the cruel orphanage. If he could survive after working in that facility filled with horrors along-side his mentor, he could handle anything that might arise in Templeton.

"Daydreaming?" Pap asked when the stagecoach came to a halt.

John opened his eyes and whispered, "I wish." He nodded to the large white building standing before them. "This is it?" He squinted and studied the steeple rooftop, the large bell hanging up above, and the cross painted on the wooden door. "I thought you said we were going to a schoolhouse. This is a church."

"Actually, it's both. School through the week for the kids in town, and on Sundays and special events, it's a church fer the rest of us."

"How . . . practical," Dr. Carson retorted, carefully stand-ing, leery that the broken-down wagon would crumble under one false move. "I intend to get to work directly, but before I do, I would like to be assured of your abilities to take my be-longings to my house."

"Oh, don't you worry about that," Pap promised, walking around to the back of his stagecoach. "I'll get out the medi-cine you brought with you and unpack the rest of your things down at Dr. Bethel's old clinic for you."

"Clinic?" John gasped. "What on earth are you talking about? When I was asked to come out to this small town and be your doctor, having a house already waiting for me was part of the agreement," he fumed, digging into his pocket for a copy of the contract. "It says right there," he continued, pointing an-grily at the written words, "that the town rallied together and built a nice home for the doctor to live in, as a thank-you for all the services provided."

"No use shovin' that thing at me." Pap yawned and tossed it back to him. "I can't read writin', can't write readin'. Now, you just cool down, young feller. Why you carryin' that thing around anyway? Don't you trust people to their word?"

"I most certainly do not!" he proclaimed bitterly. "When you do, things like *this* happen."

"You don't need to get all mad, son. You're gonna get your house, I promise. But just not right now, that's all."

John crossed his arms. "And just why not?"

"Well, Sarah's still living there. Dr. Bethel's daughter, the one I told you about. With her pa just dyin', we ain't had time to get her settled somewhere else. We all just guessed that you would understand and stay at the clinic until this outbreak is over. Sarah hasn't even had time to think about figurin' what she's gonna do now that her pa's gone. She's been too busy treatin' the sick. If you'd just stay at the clinic until this is all over, she'd have time to figure it out. Please try to understand."

"I do understand," John replied haughtily. "Many people lose the ones they love, and it's unfortunate, but it happens. You don't get time to plan out your future while the rest of world stays on hold just for you."

"Course not," Pap agreed. "But this is special. And, well, if you don't stay at the clinic . . . I just don't think I have the heart to tell Sarah. I don't even know where she would go."

"To the clinic, that's where," John answered. "If it's good enough for the new doctor, it's good enough for the daughter of the old one. And as for telling Miss Sarah Bethel, if you don't have the heart to tell her, you won't have to. I'll tell her, I won't mind at all."

"Tell me what?" a tired voice asked as the doors of the schoolhouse opened and a young woman stepped into the sunlight.

For a moment, John found himself speechless. He squinted, staring at the beautiful girl. Though her striking features were laced with fatigue, and her honey-colored blond hair was in a tangled braid, she was a captivating lady and prettier than any woman he had ever seen in Boston.

"You're Sarah Bethel?" John stammered.

"I am," she answered, her voice soft and weary. "I'm assuming you are Dr. John Carson from Saint Francis Hospital in Boston, correct?"

"Correct," John responded, vividly impressed by her grammar. She sounded nothing like Pap Dickens. Her voice wasn't identical to the tones he was accustomed to hearing in New England, but it was a pleasant surprise.

Even her body language was completely different. She walked delicately, with her shoulders pushed back like all the regal women in Boston did, lifting her skirt to keep the hem of her dress from dragging against the dirty ground, unlike Mrs. North. In fact, it was only the simple and tattered yellow frock she wore that made her look like she belonged in this rural town.

Sarah offered him a wan smile when she came closer. "Welcome. I hope your journey was a comfortable one and not too long. I'm glad you have finally arrived here. I'm afraid I desperately need your help."

"Pleasure to meet you, Miss Bethel," John said and tipped his hat to her. "My journey was tolerable, for the most part," he informed her, casting a quick glare at Pap's torturous wagon. "And I will be happy to help you restore your town to health."

"Naturally, I want you to get to work immediately, but I overheard that you have something to tell me. I'm just hoping the medicine you brought with you wasn't damaged during your trip."

"Oh, nothing of the sort," Dr. Carson assured her.

Briefly, he wondered if he should be so bold as to request that Sarah abandon her home and relocate to the clinic. She clearly was a refined, classy lady. Surely, she would understand his desire to have a house of his own, and understand that a promise was something to be kept, no matter what circumstances came with it.

"Well, you see—" he began.

"Wait!" Pap called out, gathering the suitcases filled with medicine and walking toward the schoolhouse as quickly as his old, skinny legs would allow. "I don't want to be around to watch this."

"Very well." John sighed, clearly confused. But he supposed this was normal behavior for such an eccentric old man. "Sarah," he said steadily, "as you know, the town built a house that is strictly meant for the doctor."

Sarah nodded. "Yes, it's a lovely home. My father and I were always happy there."

"I'm very glad that you were. But, sadly, your father is no longer with us. When I agreed to come here, I was promised a house of my own. Now, I did not know, nor did I realize that home is the same one you are still living in. I understand that it will probably be very hard for you to leave, considering the memories you have there, but I can tell that you are a very intelligent woman. And, of course, you would be—all nurses are. But, despite your loss, I believe I should be entitled to live in the home that was promised to me."

"Oh, is that what you think?" Sarah asked through clenched teeth, her lovely sapphire blue eyes darkening in anger. "You just roll into town and expect me to leave the only home I have ever known, just because it was promised to you? Do you even care what becomes of me?"

"Well, yes, I do expect you to follow the agreement and give me the home. And I do care about what becomes of you. Pap had mentioned lodging at the clinic, and I would be more than happy to allow you to stay at my clinic, free of charge. It's the least I can do for the daughter of the former town doctor, and my nurse."

"The clinic?" Sarah gasped. "I most certainly will not be staying at that clinic, and neither will you! I have not moved out of my father's home, because I have not stepped foot in that house for weeks. My home has been here," she explained, roughly gesturing at the schoolhouse. "I've been here night and day for weeks, trying to keep everyone as healthy as I can, even after my own father died! I haven't had time to grieve, or even think of moving my things into the clinic so that the precious new doctor could have my house!"

John gulped, suddenly understanding why Pap Dickens had been in such a hurry to get away before he told Sarah his plan. Who knew this repulsive, juvenile temper rested in such an attractive woman with a regal façade.

Swiftly, he cleared his throat, refusing to let anyone change his plans and take away the house that had been promised to him. "Just calm down, we don't need to behave like immature children over this. As you mentioned, for the time being, I will be here at the schoolhouse with the sick townspeople. After we have this dilemma under control, you can then move your things into the clinic, and I'm willing to help. I will allow you to leave some of your belongings at the house for safekeeping until you have a permanent and practical arrangement."

"You'll *allow* me?" Sarah mocked, throwing her head back. "How kind of you, Dr. Carson. You're practically as generous as a saint. That will not be necessary. I would rather live in a barn filled with animals than stay in a house or a clinic that you claim is yours."

"Animals," John laughed. "You're intelligent and funny. Remember, you will have to be at the clinic. You're a nurse."

"Yes, animals," Sarah hissed. "Besides, they couldn't be as dirty and heartless as you are! And where are you coming up with this nurse nonsense?"

"Pap," John answered simply. "He told me you had been

treating the ill people in town and had even made a refuge for them. I just presumed you were a nurse."

Sarah heaved an angry breath. "I am not a nurse. I've never had medical schooling. Pap Dickens is just a sweet old man, and he has always been very fond of me. In his eyes, I am a nurse. I am to everyone in town. I have been helping my father all my life. He trained me."

"I don't even have a nurse!" Dr. Carson complained angrily, stomping his foot into the ground, swearing when he realized the streets were not made of cobblestone and dust clung to his shoes. "I get some hand-me-down helper! How am I supposed to depend on you for any assistance? You're probably not even able to read a book on modern medicine, let alone practice it."

"I may not be a nurse," Sarah admitted, locking eyes with the complaining doctor, "but I was honored to help my father. And it's an insult to his memory to let the people in Templeton see that the doctor I requested is a snobby, rude city boy like you! You don't need to worry about the house. I'll gladly move out. And you can have the clinic. I have no idea where I'll go, but I'm sure wherever it is, it will be better than being near you! And—"

Suddenly, Sarah retreated into silence, turning her head toward the schoolhouse, when she heard a small voice calling out her name.

"Oh, Milly must be awake," she muttered. "Come on," she said, facing Dr. Carson. "You may be a snobby man, but you're the only doctor we have now."

Angrily, John followed Sarah up the creaky steps, but found his anger short-lived when he glanced inside the schoolhouse, his breath taken away by the sordid sight. The floor was invisible, covered with the bodies of sick children and adults, their faces bright red from fever, eyes dazed and bloodshot, skin bathed in perspiration. Sounds of hacking coughs hung in the air, echoing off the walls.

A lump formed in his throat. It was like seeing those ill, dying children in the orphanage all over again, and the forgotten people in Boston who were tossed into asylums and left on the streets. But now there were even more people, more people than he imagined the tiny town could have. He couldn't save them all, not on his own.

Slowly, he walked through the building, struggling to find enough room for his feet between all of the ill townspeople. Before him, Sarah knelt down to the ground and gently wiped the forehead of a frightened young child with a damp cloth.

"It's okay, Milly," she promised in a whisper. "Do you remember the doctor I told you about, the one who would come and make you all better?"

"Yes," the little girl mumbled between hacking coughs.

"Look," Sarah said softly, pointing to John. "He's here now; it's going to be all right, honey. You just calm down and rest, because getting upset will only make the fever worse. I have to go now, but Dr. Carson is going to take really good care of you, and all the children here, okay?"

"No!" Milly cried out, clinging to Sarah's hand. "No, Sarah! I want you!"

"Stay," Dr. Carson interjected as he knelt down on the opposite side of the ill child.

Sarah drew in a ragged deep breath and her eyes narrowed when she faced him. "I can't. Apparently, I have packing to do."

"We'll discuss the house later. Eventually, we'll figure it out. But for now," John said, pressing his hand to Milly's burning forehead, "some things are more important."

Chapter Two

Sarah had to use every ounce of her willpower to focus on
the ill child lying in her arms, being soothed by the gentle
touch of Sarah's hand as she dabbed her worn, feverish body
with cool water. But no matter how hard she tried, she couldn't
keep herself from gazing at the new doctor with a mixture of
relief and anger.

He had come into town with extremely high expectations
and confidence in himself, sneering at his humble surroundings and ordering her to vacate her home. He looked like he
had stepped out of one of her father's paintings of eastern
cities, dressed conservatively in a blue suit that appeared to
have been tailor-made to fit his tall, solid frame. Of all the doctors in the eastern part of the country, why did this conceited
man have to be the one to come and replace her father?

She couldn't help but feel confused while she watched John
dive into his work. He went from patient to patient quickly, his
face tense in concentration as he observed the various symptoms among them. He appeared to be making mental notes

while he worked, separating the severe and mild cases in the large group.

John Carson seemed to have completely changed since he entered the schoolhouse and saw the horror that she had been dealing with daily. The look of disgust on his face had been replaced by concern, compassion, and even fear. The complaining, ranting doctor had surprisingly been silenced.

But despite the relief that washed over her, Sarah still wasn't at ease with the young, mysterious doctor of multiple moods. She knew that once the epidemic was over, no matter what the outcome might be, the greedy man would once again bring up the house. And the fierce determination that shone in his dark eyes was a constant reminder that he would never give up the home that had been promised to him.

Sarah bit down on her lip, deep in thought as she rewet the damp cloth in her hand and pressed it to Milly's red face. Why did he care so much about claiming the house? Never in all her years had she seen an unmarried young man so determined to have a large home of his own. He had no wife or children to care for. Why couldn't he live at the clinic temporarily? The single bedroom would be pleasant enough for his bachelor lifestyle.

In annoyance, Sarah grimaced. Then again, why couldn't *she* live at the clinic happily? She, too, was unmarried and without children. But unlike Dr. Carson, the house out in the countryside held many memories for her and just enough land for her beloved horse, Thunder, that she had owned since her childhood, to run freely.

"I'll need more supplies," Dr. Carson said sharply, breaking into her scattered thoughts. "I don't have enough materials here with me to even try to begin getting this all under control," he explained as he looked over his medical bags and the boxes filled with supplies and books. "Do you have any more items here?"

"No, but there are some at my father's clinic. More people

have come in today with the fever and we're running short-handed. Mrs. North comes occasionally to bring food for me and the others when she's not busy at the post office, and I was hoping to send her to the clinic to bring more. As you can see," she whispered, looking through the crowded room, "I couldn't very well go myself."

"Of course not," John replied. "Pap!" he called out, and gestured to the old man hidden in the corner, making funny faces and ridiculous noises at the sick children quarantined in the schoolhouse in a weak hope of bringing a smile to their faces.

Upon hearing his name, Pap immediately stopped and carefully made his way through the narrow space toward the doctor. "What can I do for ya, kid?"

"I need you to go to the clinic and get some supplies. Could you do that?"

Pap straightened his straw hat with pride. "You bet I can!"

"Bring back as much as you can fit into your wagon," John requested. "Though, I don't know how in the world we'll make it fit in this crowded place."

Watching Pap walk out the door on his way to the clinic, Sarah felt a sudden wave of sadness at the thought of someone else using the instruments that had only been held in her father's hands. She shut her eyes and covered her weary face to hide the tears that threatened to spill over onto her pale cheeks. Having Dr. John Carson here, tending to her neighbors who had fallen ill, made her desperately miss her father and the many times she had assisted him.

Never again would she be at his side, helping a sick father heal so he could return to his fields or watching a mother give birth to a new child. Her father had always been her shield, determined to protect her from harm and try to lessen the pain that came from the absence of her mother. He had been her teacher, unfazed by the unwillingness of society to let women practice medicine, and taught his daughter everything he knew.

Sarah had never allowed herself to grieve the loss of such an amazing man. She had been far too busy to let herself fall into a depression and leave the sick townspeople unattended. She had to do her best to keep the rest of Templeton alive and well and show that the trust her father had left in her hands had not been unwarranted.

As she turned her head, she gazed at the faces of friends and neighbors, faces she had known all her life. But they weren't the same. They were weak and weary. Tiredly, Sarah glanced at John Carson's face—the face of the new doctor she had once believed would be the answer to her prayer, but who had only brought her more problems with his self-indulgent desire to take away her job and her home. And even though she was surrounded by people, sandwiched into the old schoolhouse so tightly she could barely move, Sarah had never felt more alone.

"Are you all right?" John asked from behind, his voice a whisper.

"Fine," she told him curtly, embarrassed that the uppity doctor had found her in such a state. Now was the time to prove her abilities and make him realize how horribly wrong he had been about her. She may not have been a nurse, but she knew she was just as capable as anyone with a nursing education, and probably had more experience than most graduates.

Roughly, she cleared her throat and dried her eyes before facing him. "I'm afraid my eyes are getting tired, perhaps from the strain of the past few days."

"That could easily happen to someone who has not been professionally trained and taught to deal with the chaos of an epidemic."

Sarah bit her tongue and fought the urge to give in to her temper. For just a moment, she had sensed a touch of kindness in the doctor's voice, and just as quickly as it had come, it vanished.

"But we don't have time to dwell on our inadequate surroundings," Dr. Carson continued rapidly. "How's Milly doing?"

"Finally asleep," Sarah said in relief as she pushed the little girl's matted brown curls off her forehead with her fingertips. "The fever has gone down just a bit from the cool cloths, but I'm afraid it will just be as high as it was before when she wakes."

John nodded grimly in agreement. "I'm afraid you're right. Have you been able to cure anyone?"

"Just a few adults have seemed to get better on their own with due time. But there has also been another death since Pap left to get you." She shook her head. "Every time I think things might be under control, everything just crumbles again."

"It's to be expected when you have no method of treating people besides wet rags to break a fever. I wonder if I might speak with you about our options, outside perhaps." He wiped his heavily perspiring brow. "It's sweltering in here."

"Do you think it's safe to leave them? What if something happens while we're outside?"

"We'll only be on the steps of the church," John reminded her, leaning over one of the boxes he had brought with him to retrieve a book. "Besides, what good will either of us be to the others if we're dehydrated and exhausted? Part of practicing medicine is caring for yourself."

"I suppose you're right," Sarah answered quietly, wishing that her father had considered doing that for himself.

Slowly, she followed the doctor out of the schoolhouse, shutting the door and breathing a sigh of relief to have a moment away from the horrible sights and sounds inside. She sat down on the steps and took a deep breath, savoring the fresh air. Even though she had just been outside to greet Pap and the new doctor, she had been too focused on meeting Dr. Carson and explaining the grave situation facing Templeton to enjoy the brief absence from the four walls of the schoolhouse.

The cool wind whipped through her braided hair and ruffled the leaves in the trees in the schoolyard. Narrowing her blue eyes, she gazed at the leaves above her. She had been so busy and secluded from normal everyday life, she hadn't even noticed that they were changing from green to shades of gold and red, announcing the arrival of fall.

Unwillingly, she faced John, knowing her moments of relaxation would pass quickly. "What did you want to talk about? Are you wanting to discuss the house *now*?"

John grimaced as he removed his blue hat and jacket to thoroughly enjoy the breeze. "Not yet. But it will be discussed, I assure you." He passed her the book he had retrieved inside. "But more importantly, I wanted to ask you if you had any knowledge of this."

"Homeopathy?" Sarah read slowly.

"Yes, are you familiar with it?" John questioned.

She shook her head. "Not really. I've only heard of it a little, when Papa would talk about it from time to time. But he never practiced it. Isn't it the practice of natural healing?"

"Something like that. If I understand correctly, homeopathy will stimulate self-healing. You see, patients are given a medication that would cause a healthy, robust person to fall ill. However, if the person has already taken ill and has begun to show symptoms, the substance could actually help them regain their strength and get better. The medications are made from natural things that surround us, such as plants, animals, or minerals."

Sarah paused a moment and tried to fully digest Dr. Carson's words as she quickly skimmed over the book's pages. "It sounds like fighting fire with fire."

"Precisely," John told her, beginning to pace back and forth over the grass. "Treating like with like. It sounds completely foolish at first, but I have seen it work. While I was training with Dr. Thompson, I saw him apply homeopathic treatments when we were dealing with an epidemic of our own."

"And was this Dr. Thompson a specialist in the field?"

He bowed his head. "No, but he was an incredible doctor and an even better man. He wasn't too proud to look outside the boundaries of conventional medicine. And in the end, the alternative techniques provided a greater recovery rate than the ones used in the local hospitals."

Sarah sat silently for a moment, at a loss for words after witnessing the self-assured doctor speak so highly of someone other than himself. "There really was a difference?" she whispered, fearful of raising her hopes.

"Yes, as unbelievable as it sounds, there was. And I believe this may be our only way to get a handle on the epidemic here."

A small grin spread over Sarah's lips when she gazed down at the path John's endless pacing had sketched into the grass, as he grew more and more excited by the idea of homeopathy. There was a different presence about him now as he spoke of medicine and his old mentor with such reverence and excitement, as if he had tossed aside his haughty attitude along with his hat and jacket.

His dark eyes that had appeared nearly black with anger had softened to their natural brown, and his wavy, dark blond hair was disheveled from the wind, almost giving him an approachable, handsome quality as he stood preparing a plan for Templeton. And despite still being uncertain of his strange and inconsistent personality, Sarah was elated to have found something likable about him. He appeared to be a devoted doctor who was willing to push aside his conventional training to pursue whatever means of treatment would best benefit his patients.

"What's the treatment for scarlet fever?" she questioned. "Using homeopathy, what's the recommended material?"

John slowly ended his pacing and stood stiffly. He lifted his head. "Belladonna," he answered quietly. "It's a plant."

"I know what it is," Sarah snapped, crossing her arms. "It's not just a plant. My papa called it "devil's cherries" and said it was dangerous. You must be out of your mind if you think I will stand here and let you give deathly sick people a poisonous plant! Devil's cherries can kill a healthy person; it's certain death for someone who's already sick."

"No, it's not," John assured her, his voice steady and firm. "I know it must sound silly. It did to me at first. But you have to trust me. The whole idea of homeopathy is treating symptoms with things that would cause them in healthy people. For some reason, unknown to me and most of the medical world, the disease seems to deteriorate."

She glared up at him. "You're admitting you don't understand this?"

"I'm admitting my knowledge is limited. I'm not trained in homeopathy, and when I assisted Dr. Thompson with the treatments, I was barely fourteen years old, practically a child. That's why I've brought along so much literature on the subject."

"Who cares what books you brought? None of it matters if you don't really understand the core reason behind the information inside. How can you be willing to practice something you barely understand?"

"Sarah, I'm willing because my conventional ways rarely work, and I've seen the statistics of a radical method that has. I figure if this sort of thing has been good enough for royal families in Europe to have been using for years and years, it is good enough for us to try here."

Sarah felt her pulse doubling and she wondered if she could control her raging temper. "So I suppose Templeton is the perfect place to begin testing homeopathy to see how it really works. Who cares if it kills a few backward folks? They're not as important as fine ladies and gentlemen like you."

"I didn't mean that," John shot back. "All I want to do is

eradicate this epidemic before it gets even worse. I'm just trying to find a way to prevent the horrible outcomes I've seen."

Sarah felt flabbergasted. How could she allow this new doctor to fill the mouths of townspeople with a medication created from a plant she knew to be deadly? But yet, how could she continue treating people with methods she knew were barely working and often only temporary?

"I'm not brave enough to risk it," she finally said in a hesitant whisper. "You should stick to the practices you were taught and used in Boston. It's safer. Those are the same procedures I saw my father give and assisted with."

"And they're the same ways that get us nowhere," John argued. "I'm trying to let you have a say. Even if I think it is ridiculous for an uneducated woman, who is considered to be as intelligent as a nurse merely because her father was the town doctor, to be treating anyone, I can see that everyone here trusts you. If you have faith in what I'm doing, so will they."

Sarah pondered his words. He was right. Everyone in town trusted her right now—the only thing more secure than her word was the Gospel. Perhaps if she just pretended to trust Dr. Carson's idea, the sick bodies lying in the schoolhouse would do the same. If the remedy didn't cure them, maybe newfound hope would create enough strength to buy time to try a more conservative route that would.

"Well?" John prodded, growing anxious and returning to his pacing.

"I think—"

Sarah's answer was quickly silenced by the sound of horse hooves rushing over the ground. Turning her head, she saw a wagon coming quickly toward them, swaying dangerously from side to side as it topped each hill.

"Who is that alarming driver?" John asked in disgust.

"Ned Gibson," Sarah said with a sudden catch in her throat, as he approached and she could see the terrified look that glazed over his eyes. "Lord, please don't let May be sick," she prayed, murmuring her best friend's name.

"Sarah!" Ned called out in a panic as he jumped down to the ground, not even taking a moment to catch his breath. "You gotta help me! May's sick!" he hollered as he ran to the bed of the wagon.

Without a word, Sarah followed, thankful when she heard John's footsteps echoing behind her. Tears misted her eyes when she reached her friend.

Lying in back of the wagon, covered in tattered blankets, May Taylor lay shivering uncontrollably. Her chest heaved up and down rapidly, her breath releasing tightly, as though being forced. Her freckles were hidden under the bright crimson color that spread over her face, and her brown hair was darkened and matted to her forehead from the constant perspiring.

"Sarah," she gasped, weakly reaching out to her with a trembling hand. "Sarah, are you there?"

Sarah gripped her fingers. "I'm right here. I'm right here with you, May."

"I'm scared," May choked out as tears flooded her dreary eyes. "I don't—I don't want to die. . . ."

"You won't die," Sarah interjected firmly. "We've got a doctor here now, and neither of us will let you die."

Dr. Carson stepped forward and wrapped his arms underneath May. "Let's move her inside!" he ordered.

"Whoa, wait just a dern second, feller! What do ya think you're doin', grabbin' her like that?" Ned hissed.

"Ned, calm down," Sarah demanded calmly. "This is Dr. Carson. He was just going to carry May inside."

Ned roughly brushed passed John and lifted May into his arms. "Oh, well . . . I'll do that myself, thank ye very much."

"I don't know how in the world we're going to make room for her," John worried aloud as they all hurried back inside.

"We're just going to have to make room," Sarah insisted. "I can move things around. I'll find a way to make it work."

"No," John replied, squinting his eyes to peer through the overcrowded room. "Let Ned and me tend to that; we might need to physically move a few people around. You go and get some cool, wet cloths so we can try to lower her fever. Blast! I just wish Pap would hurry up and get here with the rest of the supplies so I could start giving *some* type of medicine!"

Casting one last glance at May lying lifelessly in Ned's arms and Dr. Carson gently rousing some of the sleeping patients, Sarah grabbed a few of the spare rags lying in an empty basin and headed out to the water pump.

Fear ate away at her as she stepped outside, surprised to find her own footsteps weak and shaky. She couldn't stand to lose another person she loved. Death had already taken her mother at her birth and now her father. She simply didn't know if she could survive the death of her best friend too.

But May wasn't going to die; she just couldn't. She was in her prime, ready to be married to Ned and start a family soon. All of her dreams were so close and now suddenly seemed so far.

Quickly, Sarah thrust her hand up and down, waiting anxiously for water to appear and come crashing down into the basin. The water trickled out slowly at first, then came faster as she steadily pumped. Drawing in a deep breath, she filled her hands with the cold water and splashed her face, hoping to calm down and regain the composure she would need to help May.

"Sarah! Sarah!" Pap called out in his thick twang, his voice echoing over the hills as he came into sight. "I got it here for y'all!"

"Oh, bless you, Pap!" Sarah praised, setting the basin to the ground.

"I went as quick as I could," Pap told her as he brought his rickety wagon to a halt.

"You did just fine! Let me help you get these things inside."

"Ah, now you may be one smart gal, Sarah Bethel, but there's still some things a man just don't let a woman fuss with. You just carry that bowl on back inside and I'll take care of this load."

Sarah rolled her blue eyes but managed a smile at Pap's stubborn ways. Peering at her father's medical supplies scattered in the wagon, she noticed a foreign bag lying in the corner.

"Where did you find that bag?" she asked, pointing with her finger.

"Oh, that musta been left over. It's one of the new doc's. I'll be back for it in a minute," Pap promised as he carried in the first load.

Letting her curiosity get the better of her, Sarah untied the twine keeping the bag closed. She lifted one of the bottles lying inside and read the handwritten label. *Belladonna.*

Without a moment of hesitation, she grasped the bottle and ran back into the schoolhouse. Carefully, she made her way to Dr. Carson as he sat in the corner, examining May.

"Did you bring the wet rags?" he asked, never taking his gaze away from his newest patient.

"No, I brought this," Sarah whispered, holding out the bottle.

John raised his head and locked eyes with her. "You want me to try homeopathy?"

Sarah turned her head and gazed at all the motionless bodies covering the floor, then looked back at her own best friend fighting for her life.

"I don't think we have a choice."

Chapter Three

John Carson lay still, allowing his eyes to remain shut even though he couldn't manage to sleep, savoring the refuge the dark of night briefly provided against the ongoing epidemic. Another two days had passed and there had yet to be any improvement. More people had begun showing symptoms of scarlet fever and more people had succumbed to it, including Milly, the little girl who had been the first patient he'd seen in Templeton. He had begun to fear he was fighting a battle that he would never win.

The helplessness ate away at him, leaving him frustrated and morose as he recalled his earlier years back in Boston, when he was alone and too young to help himself or others avoid the cruelty, crime, and disease of the city streets. What would Dr. Thompson have thought if he'd seen the people whom John had been unable to help, after all the years he had dedicated to teaching John to treat the downtrodden?

Unable to allow himself another minute of rest, John opened his weary eyes and pulled himself to his feet. He knew all too well that if he allowed any more thoughts to invade his restless mind, memories of his own haunting past would follow and sleep would never come.

His dark eyes roamed the crowded schoolhouse and gazed at the sleeping patients, and he was thankful to have so many make it through another night. Squinting, he searched the masses, hoping to see Sarah sleeping among them.

Over the past forty-eight hours, he had yet to see the resilient young woman sleep. Whenever he woke from the meager naps he managed, he would find her comforting a patient with a lullaby or soothing words, monitoring a fever, or checking the record kept on old chalkboard slates of the doses given of belladonna.

But this time he found Sarah kneeling at the window, her shoulders sagging from exhaustion and her hands clasped firmly over her heart as she murmured a quiet prayer. John stood rigidly, captivated by the display of open faith that only added to her beauty. He envied her. She seemed so confident that someone could hear her pleas and provide help to her poor town. If only he could learn to trust someone to help him when he needed it most.

Sarah opened her sapphire eyes and gasped when she saw him standing only a few feet from her. "I—Is everything all right, Dr. Carson?"

"Fine," he answered briskly. "I hope I didn't interrupt your moment with the Lord."

"Oh, I wasn't talking to the Lord. Naturally, I talk to the Lord, as any good woman should, but I was talking to my father. Prayer is the only way I can now."

"I suppose we do need all the help we can get," John commented evenly in an attempt to keep his skepticism from seeping into his words.

"I was asking him to watch over Milly." She rubbed her forehead and took a ragged breath. "And all the others who are approaching death's door."

"Sarah, I know the last several hours have been daunting. But things, for the moment at least, are calmer and I can handle the situation solo. Perhaps you should lie down and try to rest while everyone seems to be quiet and there's still a few hours left of the night."

"It's pointless," Sarah replied wearily. "I can't seem to turn off all the thoughts running through my mind. If I shut my eyes, they only get louder."

Dr. Carson nodded his head sympathetically. At times, the thoughts and memories running through his mind seemed louder than a roaring canyon: the crude people who lived in the boardinghouse with him in Boston, the doctors and his colleagues at Saint Francis Hospital who looked down upon him because his last name wasn't linked to wealth, the faces of the children still trapped in the awful orphanages and asylums whom he and his mentor could no longer care for.

"What do you think about?" he asked.

"I worry about so many things. Why Papa didn't make it. And if I live through this epidemic, where will I go when it's all over? But those aren't the thoughts that keep me awake. It's worrying about the rest of the town and May that does. Sometimes, I wonder if the schoolyard will disappear," Sarah whispered abruptly as she stared off into the distance, pointing at the graveyard. "Did you ever worry about things like that when Boston was suffering with an epidemic, Dr. Carson? Worrying that soon there might be more new graves than old?"

John approached the window and drew in a breath while he gazed at the old tombstones and freshly dug graves just beyond the church, shadowed by the night. "I never really thought about it in Boston. There are so many people and so many faces, it is fairly simple not to be attached. If one person dies, you simply make room for the next patient you hope you can save. I know it sounds heartless, but that's just the way things are in crowded hospitals."

Sarah faced him and meekly asked, "Even when children die?"

As the question left her lips, John felt his stomach explode into a dozen knots being pulled in each direction. It was as if she looked through him and saw the horrible memories of the city streets, asylums, and orphanages that he was trying so hard to forget. "Yes, even children, I suppose," he replied, struggling to keep his voice steady.

Sarah cast her gaze out the window once more. "Maybe it's different when you know the children and adults being put into the ground. Only days ago, Milly was clinging to my hand and calling my name. She begged me not to leave her—maybe I should have begged her not to leave *me*. Telling her mama and papa their little girl didn't make it through the night nearly hurt more than losing my father. I know it might be different for you. Maybe there are too many new faces to remember one little girl."

"No, I remember," he retorted quietly. He had seen countless sick bodies when he stepped into the schoolhouse, but once he had stared into Milly's flushed face, her innocent, frightened expression reminded him it was time to cast aside his thoughts about his house and focus on being a good doctor. "She had a little round face, brown curls, and wide eyes."

"Yes," she murmured.

John peered down at her from the corner of his eye, seeing that her eyes were free of tears, even though her voice cracked with emotion. And he instinctively knew it was only because Sarah no longer had any tears left to shed.

"There's nothing worse than a funeral for a child," she added.

John leaned heavily against the wall, remembering the sobs of Milly's parents ringing through the schoolhouse. He had never heard such a cry in his life.

"How many more will be buried?" Sarah asked as she looked around the crowded room. "I had hoped and prayed that things would get better when you arrived, but people are still dying. How long will it be until the graveyard is full and the schoolhouse is empty?"

"Sarah, you can't let yourself think that way. This isn't over yet; things might get better. The homeopathic treatments I'm using haven't had time to begin reversing the symptoms yet."

"They might not do any good. We both know that. In your book it said it works best when people get belladonna immediately. We have people here who have been sick for days and days. It was too late for Milly and probably too late for a lot of other people too."

John paused, unable to offer any uplifting words. "Naturally, more people will die, it's a sad fact. There will be more graves, but there's no way for us to tell how many will be needed until everything is finally over."

Sarah sat silently for a moment and studied him with a quzzical expression. "You've changed so much since you stepped into this schoolhouse. Your righteous attitude has nearly disappeared. Why are you trying so hard to save my town? A town I know you find simple-minded and dull."

"It's part of being a doctor," John answered plainly, forcing himself not to gaze into her pretty face that even fatigue couldn't alter. "Whether I'm in Templeton or a castle, I am expected to treat patients to the best of my ability. Besides, like it or not, this is my home now and the people in it are my patients. I should start getting used to it."

" 'Like it or not'?" she quoted. "If your old personality is going to come back once this epidemic is over, I'd prefer you catch the next train to Boston. The people in this town have been through enough. They don't need to be dealing with a doctor who thinks little of them on top of it."

Amy Blizzard

Upon hearing the anger lacing Sarah's words, John actually found himself fighting off a smile. It felt good to hear the vibrant, powerful spirit that thrived in her coming to life again.

"I wouldn't belittle my own patients. It will just take time. Eventually, everyone will adjust to me."

"Maybe you should adjust to them," she countered.

"I'm sorry, but I can't imagine myself ever adjusting to people like Pap Dickens."

"And why not? Maybe that old man is a bit odd, but you could never meet a nicer person. He took off at a moment's notice to get you from the train station and he wouldn't even accept your money for the ride. When we needed more supplies, he was right back in that rickety wagon of his. I know he's getting old and tired, but he won't even think of letting it show, because he doesn't want people to be afraid to ask for a favor. Tell me, Dr. Carson, is it so hard to adjust to a man like that?"

"No, I suppose not. But why does he do all those favors? And why do people ask him? Surely, there must be strong boys in town who could help the postal woman with a broken fence."

"People ask because they see how happy he is after he helps someone. It's what keeps him young at heart. And as for Mrs. North," Sarah explained with a smile, "she never really has anything that needs to be fixed. Her biggest problem is her loneliness. She's a widow and Pap's been helping her ever since her husband passed. Everyone knows they're sweet on each other, but Mrs. North still loves Mr. North too much to ever admit how much she cares for old Pap."

"And what about Pap? Why doesn't he say anything?"

"Because he's too darn stubborn for his own good, that's why," Sarah answered, shaking her head. "That's a man for you. Papa was just as stubborn, only his stubbornness cost him his life. And I'm just as much to blame. I knew he was sick."

"You shouldn't bother wasting time blaming yourself," John told her. "You and I may have found something we agree on: men are stubborn."

"That doesn't matter," she replied wearily. "This wasn't just a man. It was my father. If it had been me, there wouldn't have been any debate. He would've made me stop trying to help immediately so I could be taken care of."

"I'd do the same if you took ill," he stated softly, surprising himself with the gentleness in his tone.

"I've never been sick a day in my life," Sarah said quickly, seeming to be equally startled by his random compassion. "You won't have to worry about it."

"Good. I have superior immunity as well."

"I guess we should get back to work and go check on everyone," Sarah announced distractedly. "We've been chatting for far too long."

"Let them sleep," John retorted, sighing. "If the belladonna isn't working as a cure, it may be working as a sedative, and sleep is the only thing that might bring any of them comfort now."

"Are you restless often, Dr. Carson?"

"Only during times like these. You?"

"The same, I guess. I never had a problem until now. I don't even remember how to fall asleep."

"Eventually, you'll remember," John promised. "In time, your body will take over your mind's worries and your eyes will stay shut."

"You sound very experienced. Are you used to worrying?"

"All doctors are. You go to bed worrying, as Dr. Thompson used to say. I'm sure you know about that from your father."

"A little," Sarah acknowledged. "I'm sure you're not the only one with worries. You must have family back East trembling from fright because you took off to come out here in the middle of a scarlet fever outbreak."

John retreated into silence, growing more and more uncomfortable from Sarah's casual questioning. For a moment, he was tempted to make a snide remark that would cause her to loathe him once again and never ask another question. But the thought of the beautiful young woman never speaking another word to him felt nearly as painful as his protected past.

"You certainly are talkative today," he commented slowly, hoping he could change the subject and continue the conversation. "I had grown accustomed to you ignoring me."

"I'd love to ignore you," Sarah stated frankly. "I'd love to pretend you never came, my town wasn't taken prisoner by this epidemic, my father was alive, and you weren't vying for my house. But I would only be fooling myself. You're here now, and even if we won't be working together in my father's clinic, we'll still have to be together to work out the details of the home. It's silly to continue acting like children, even though my temper sometimes does get the best of me. I'm sorry if I've bothered you with our chattering. I didn't intend to. I was just growing tired of silence being my only companion at night."

"You needn't apologize, Sarah. I have enjoyed speaking with you. In fact, I can't remember the last time I was able to converse with someone so easily." He swallowed roughly when she gave him a breathtaking smile. "After all," he added quickly, "I've mainly just been asking patients questions since I arrived, and during my drive here, Pap talked enough for two."

"I understand," Sarah said, standing. "It was nice to speak with you as well, but now I've got to find something productive to do. I can't bear to stay still or look out this window another minute pondering what lies ahead."

"Neither can I," John agreed. "Perhaps we could go through the clean laundry Mrs. North was kind enough to drop off?"

Sarah glanced at him suspiciously and then nodded her head. "Yes, that's a good idea."

"You look shocked. Is the thought of me having a good idea really that extreme?"

Her cheeks turned slightly rosy as she knelt to the ground and began sifting through the blankets. "No, I've just never met a man who was willing to help with laundry in any fashion, my father included."

John sat beside her and forced a wan smile. "I've done plenty of laundry in my life. I didn't have a mother to do it for me."

"Oh, I'm so sorry," Sarah apologized.

The sincerity in her words, which he had rarely heard from anyone else, touched his heart. "Thank you."

"Did you grow up with only your father as well?" she asked.

"No, my parents passed together years ago, when I was just a boy. You were wrong when you assumed there were people back in Boston worrying about me," he answered.

Why was he still telling her more? He had always fought to protect his past, and yet, when he spoke with her it felt so tempting to share every detail.

"You don't even have any friends back at the hospital?"

Dr. Carson shook his head. "Only my dear mentor, who passed a couple of years ago."

"Dr. Thompson must have been a very good man. Your voice changes when you speak of him. You mentioned that you assisted him at a very young age. Did he take you in after your parents passed?"

John bit down on his lip anxiously. He should have expected someone as bright as Sarah to begin piecing together the bits of information he had revealed. He would have to make a stronger effort to keep up his defenses. If he shared too much, he risked having her look at him with the pity and disgust that had laced the stares he'd received back in Boston.

"No, he didn't take me in while I was a boy, but he did help me restart my life," he recalled, running a hand over the sleeve of his fancy suit, one of Dr. Thompson's many hand-me-downs. "Without him, I know I never could have been a doctor." He took a breath and added so softly Sarah could not hear, "I don't know if I would even be alive."

"It's nice to know there were such good doctors in Boston. Were your other co-workers as kind?"

"I never really got to know anyone at the facility," John answered, "because I was frequently leaving to make house calls to some of the city's forgotten patients."

"I'm glad to hear you're familiar with house calls," Sarah replied as she placed folded sheets in neat rows. "Papa made house calls very often—hopefully, you will do so as well. I wasn't aware any doctors practiced that way in the East. I thought patients were expected to make their way to private practices and hospitals."

"It depends on the amount of money in the patient's pocket," John explained bleakly. "But Dr. Thompson was a good man and taught me that sometimes the doctor has to go to the patient. He saw many of the people in the city who had been forgotten in asylums and orphanages, even street children, occasionally."

"Hearing about those places gives me chills," Sarah whispered, shuddering. "It's just so hard to believe a person can be abandoned as if he were a stray animal. You must have seen some horrible things there, Dr. Carson."

The doctor only nodded as he shut his eyes, wishing that would hide the memories. Not only had he seen the horrible things done to the city's outcasts behind closed doors, he had lived through them. He had been an orphaned child thrown into an asylum with angry, wild adults. Just another nameless orphan handed over to be an indentured servant to a couple claiming to save homeless boys.

John opened his eyes to see Sarah still trembling. "Are you all right?" he asked, worried. The awful memories abruptly vanished and were replaced by fright. What if her chills weren't brought on by sympathy, but by the beginnings of scarlet fever?

"Are you feeling ill?" he prodded, placing his palm to her forehead.

Sarah gently pulled away from his touch. "I'm fine. My shivering only came from thinking of those awful places and knowing that if I weren't here in Templeton, I very well could be one of those outcasts. I still have no idea what might happen to me, but I know that no one here would allow me to be locked away and forgotten."

"Well, I'm glad you're all right," he mumbled and turned away from her, embarrassed by his overreaction and shocked by his growing compassion for Sarah. "I suppose we should begin preparing the doses of belladonna to be given out."

"Do you really think it's working?" Sarah inquired worriedly, her voice only a whisper.

"Do you think it's hurting anyone?"

"No more than the fever," she murmured. "But it still scares me to be giving people a plant that my father had warned me about. It's hard to see the reasoning. But I know you're doing the best you can."

"I wish I could do more and had more knowledge of homeopathy."

"You shouldn't belittle your efforts," Sarah told him honestly. "You've been a great help, and it's been nice to not have to handle this all on my own anymore."

"Well, I certainly am surprised to hear you say that, Miss Sarah Bethel. You said I've changed since entering the schoolhouse, but I don't think I'm the only one. Can this possibly be the same woman sitting here, having a polite conversation with me, who not so long ago was calling me a rude, snobby city boy and wanted to lodge with barn animals to avoid me?"

Sarah gave him a weary smile. "Yes, it is. I just happened to remember the sick people here are more important than any personal issues I may have with you, Dr. Carson. Their lives are worth more than our bickering over a home and whether or not you want me to work with you in the clinic. And, quite frankly, the epidemic has finally begun to take its toll on me. I'm too fatigued to keep arguing. However, if you somehow manage to say something arrogant or egotistical, my temper could quickly surface despite exhaustion."

"I don't doubt that at all," John chuckled. "I shall try my best not to give your temper reason to return. But we both know that eventually we will have to make arrangements for ourselves."

"I know we will," Sarah said steadily. "But right now, I'm just not ready. The future of Templeton is already so uncertain, I don't even know if I'll have a town to call my own by the time this is all over. That house holds more memories than you could ever imagine, but it's only a house. If you could cure May and the rest of my neighbors, I'd hand you the key with a smile on my face. Without my friends here with me, Templeton won't be my home anymore."

As John stared into Sarah's worried eyes, he saw a little of himself. He wanted to hide from his dark past and she wanted to hide from her unknown future.

Sarah watched John quietly while he prepared the dosages of belladonna in the moonlight, intrigued by his calm demeanor. He seemed so different tonight, only a shadow of the arrogant man whom she had met just a few days ago. She brushed her fingers against her forehead, recalling his soft touch when he had checked for a fever. She should have known any man who dedicated his life to saving others couldn't be completely heartless.

"Do you need help getting the medicine ready?" she offered.

"No, I can handle it. For the past couple of days, we've developed a nice routine of you waking everyone while I get the belladonna ready for consumption. I think it's best if people wake up to a face they're familiar with, even if some of them are delirious."

Sarah smirked. "You just don't want to be griped at for disturbing someone's slumber. Especially when it comes to Caleb Patten."

"Perhaps . . ." John mumbled. "The man is worse than a grouchy bear when I wake him."

"Only due to the circumstances. When he's well, he's a gentleman and dotes on his wife, Gertie, and is eagerly preparing for the arrival of their first child."

"Well, all the same, if he's grouchy waking up to the face of a pretty girl, just imagine how awful he is when he wakes up to mine."

Pretty? Had he really just called her pretty?

Sarah stood frozen a moment, completely awestruck by his nonchalant compliment. She had been told she was attractive before by her father, Mrs. North, and May, but never by a man near her own age. All her life, the men in Templeton had only seen her as the doctor's daughter, a girl whom they would only want to call on if they were ill or injured.

With a quick shake to clear her head, Sarah turned away from Dr. Carson. If one kind word was enough to leave her flustered, her growing fatigue was making her as delirious as the feverish patients.

She walked slowly through the schoolhouse after collecting herself, feeling a pang of sadness when she stepped into each of the empty spaces on the floor and remembered the person who had been lying there only days or hours ago. She fought away tears when she reached her best friend and hoped an empty space would never replace May.

"May," Sarah said softly as she knelt down at her side. "May, wake up," she prodded and brushed her friend's brown hair aside, trying to see her face. "I need you to wake up so Dr. Carson can give you the medicine. It will only take a moment."

May moaned softly and weakly turned over.

Sarah squinted as she watched May's mane fall off her face, revealing her pale skin and freckles that had been hidden beneath the scarlet rash that had spread over her face since she had taken ill.

"May?" she gasped, placing her hand to her brow, feeling tears of joy sparkle in her eyes when her palm was greeted by cool perspiration. "Dr. Carson! Dr. Carson, come here! I think the fever's broken!"

"Sarah?" May called out, her voice a raspy whisper. "What are ya so riled up about?"

"Oh, May," Sarah whispered back as tears freely ran down her cheeks. "You've been so sick with scarlet fever, I was worried you might leave me too."

"I have scarlet fever?" May asked, managing to open her hazel eyes a little. "Oh, no, is Ned all right?"

Sarah took her hand and spoke soothingly. "Yes, Ned's fine, May. He rushed you over here just as soon as you got sick, and he wanted to be here with you very badly, but anyone who became ill was placed under quarantine. Just as soon as the doctor says everything is okay, Ned will be right here beside you again."

"I'm going to live?"

"Don't start getting gloomy now, May. You've already made it through the worst of it."

"Sarah, what's going on?" Dr. Carson inquired as he hurried toward May, digging into his medical bag while he lowered himself to the floor.

"I think her fever's broken," Sarah reported ecstatically. "She's a little confused about things that have happened recently, but she's not delirious anymore. Do you think she's getting better?"

"Let's not get too hopeful," he warned cautiously as he felt May's forehead and rested a stethoscope on her chest. "Breathe as deeply as you can, May."

"Well?" Sarah questioned anxiously, unable to keep herself calm. "She's doing better, isn't she?"

"She most certainly is," Dr. Carson replied, his eyes wide in astonishment. "The fever has broken and her lungs are clear. She's showing signs of a slow but highly possible recovery."

"The homeopathy must have worked," Sarah assumed. "You were right. Thank you!" Without thinking, Sarah wrapped her arms around him and hugged him tightly. Immediately, she was consumed with embarrassment for acting so emotionally and began to quickly pull away, but before she could, he returned the gesture. His strong arms were tense and his hesitant touch almost fearful, but somehow comforting all the same.

"Don't thank me yet," he told her and abruptly dropped his arms. "It's still too early to begin making grand assumptions. Come with me and help me check on the others. We have to evaluate everyone to truly know if the medication is working."

For the rest of the night, Sarah worked steadily at John's side, watching over the sick and praying that the rest of them would follow in May's footsteps and begin showing signs of recovery that would bring the epidemic to an end and Templeton back to life.

"They're getting better," John heard Sarah whisper as they sat together on the steps of the schoolhouse, watching the sunrise. "They're actually getting better."

"I guess miracles do happen every now and then," he admitted reluctantly, taking in a deep breath of morning air.

"Today looks quite promising. But it's still hard to know what the outcome of this outbreak might be. Unfortunately, we're almost guaranteed to lose a few more people to scarlet fever, just not as many as planned. You do understand that, don't you?"

"I do," Sarah assured him. "I know we aren't going to get a perfect ending, but I'm not afraid that graves will outnumber the living anymore. And I have you to thank. Only days ago, I sat right here arguing with you about homeopathy and devil's cherries. If I had known your radical ideas were going to save my town, I would've kept my mouth shut."

"Somehow," John said through a smile, "I just can't imagine that."

"I guess you have a point," Sarah admitted softly. "But I do want to thank you. You'll never know how much this means to me."

"You don't have to thank me," he replied, attempting to conceal his pleasure at seeing Sarah's sadness lifted. "I was only doing my job."

"There you go again. You always tell me everything you do and feel is part of being a doctor. What you accomplished here goes beyond the medical practice—some might even call it heroic."

Hearing Sarah's compliments filled John with pride and fear. He adored having Sarah look at him with new eyes, seeing past the uncouth behavior he had displayed when he first arrived, but he was worried to be seen as anything more or less than a doctor.

Being a doctor was the only thing he knew. He had never truly been a son, a brother, or even a friend. He had turned his back on being a child of the streets and an unwanted orphan. And before becoming a doctor, he had only been a student and a colleague. His mind was filled with knowledge, and his hands were trained and skilled, but he envied even the most simpleminded men who knew how to befriend and love others.

"Perhaps I have made a lot of medical references," John admitted. "But they were said in truth. I am a doctor, not a hero."

"You are to me," Sarah insisted, looking directly into his brown eyes. "I'll never be able to thank you properly. None of us will. I know you think this town is provincial, but the people here aren't. They're kind and good, and knowing that some of their lives have been spared has made the future look a little brighter. I think that qualifies as heroic," she told him in a whisper as a tear slipped down her cheek.

"Don't cry," John said gently. He reached out, with an instinct he had never felt before, and brushed her tear away with his thumb, allowing his hand to linger on her soft cheek.

It seemed hard to believe the lovely, soft-spoken woman beside him was the same woman who had bluntly shown her temper when he arrived in town. Yet, even then, Sarah had captivated him. He didn't know a woman in Boston who would have been brave enough to raise her voice to a man so easily, let alone take it upon herself to care for an entire town during a scarlet fever epidemic.

"I'm not so sure you should be filling my head with compliments," John commented and unwillingly pulled his hand back. "I'm still not positive your friend isn't suffering from delirium. She's done nothing but talk about that fiancé of hers since you woke her."

"It's perfectly normal," Sarah said, grinning. "All young women who are preparing to marry talk of nothing but their wedding and husband-to-be, especially when a wedding seemed impossible only days ago. I promised her as soon as morning came I'd go tell Ned about her progress, but I'm so tired I just don't think my legs could carry me all the way out to his farm."

"Considering you helped save her life, I think she'll forgive you. It's only sunrise now. There's still time to tell Ned."

"What do you think of the first sunrise in Templeton that

you've actually been able to view outside of the schoolhouse walls?" Sarah asked as she gazed up at the morning sky painted with shades of pink and gold.

Even though John sat at her side, he hadn't bothered to look at the rising sun. Sarah's beauty was far more captivating. Her honey-colored hair glistened in the appearing sunlight. Her blue eyes sparkled wildly and left him longing for the opportunity to touch her again and relive their awkward hug.

He had not been hugged since his childhood and had been far too young when his mother died to remember her touch. There had been thankful parents or spouses of patients who had attempted to put their arms around him, but he had always politely and professionally guided them into a handshake. But when it came to Sarah, he simply couldn't resist her charming and feminine embrace.

"Isn't it beautiful?" she asked, redirecting his attention to the sunrise. "My father used to say he never truly saw the sun rise until he came here."

"I understand what your father meant," the young doctor agreed, tilting his head to the sky. "In Boston, I rarely ever saw the sunrise. If I looked out my window in the boardinghouse, I only saw the window of another boardinghouse. And the sidewalks and city streets were always shadowed by tall buildings and hordes of people."

"Well, that's something you won't be seeing anymore. You were introduced to our small town under horrible circumstances, but soon you'll see a brighter side. You can already feel the chill in the air and see the leaves starting to change colors. Fall is arriving quickly. Once everyone is doing better, harvesting will begin. It's a wonderful time of year. The town gets together to celebrate after all the hard work is done. We have a huge barn dance and a grand meal. This year we'll have even more to celebrate. And, of course, there will be May's wedding."

John gasped and wrinkled his nose in disgust. "Harvesting? Barn dances? You mean to tell me, people here look forward to all that hard work? And they dance in a barn where animals live? Wouldn't people dance through their . . . their . . . droppings?"

"Oh, heavens no!" Sarah giggled, shaking her head. "We all get together out at the Gibson's farm, they have a lovely piece of property, and you won't have to worry about any droppings. You should come. Their farm isn't far from your house."

"*My* house?" John blurted. "Did I hear you correctly?"

"You did," Sarah murmured back. "I told you if you could save May and my neighbors, I'd give you the key to the house with a smile on my face. I intend to stay true to my word, but I do hope you'll let me do away with the smiling part. Besides, you were promised that house, weren't you?"

"Yes, I was," John replied, "but then I only saw the house as a material object. I never thought about the person who might be living there."

"I don't want your pity, Dr. Carson," Sarah said, her voice clear and strong. "Of course I'm upset. That house is the only home I have ever known, but it's time to move on. And after seeing such sickness and pain lately, I know things could be worse. After all that you've done, giving you the house without complaint is the least I can do."

John sat silently, studying the sadness in Sarah's eyes that her strong demeanor couldn't hide. He hated knowing that his desire to claim her home as his own would cause her trouble. For some reason, he worried about her.

And during the past few hours, as the two of them had begun to weaken their shields and allow part of their true selves to show, John realized why he had tried so desperately to find a way to help the ill people in Templeton, Missouri.

Naturally, as a doctor, he had wanted to cure the sick. But more than anything, he wanted to help Sarah and try to keep her from losing the friends and neighbors who were so important in her life. He didn't want her to suffer as he had.

"But what will happen to you?" he muttered abruptly. "Where will you go?"

Sarah shrugged tiredly as she pulled herself to her feet. "I'm not sure," she yawned, fighting to keep her eyes open. "But I've lost enough sleep thinking about it. It's time to take a break. You were right; eventually your body gets so tired it silences the mind's worries. Will you be able to handle everything on your own if I take a nap?"

"Yes, by all means, go rest."

Sarah nodded a silent thank-you and opened the door.

"Wait!" John called, reaching out and gently catching her hand before she went inside.

"What?" Sarah asked with a weak laugh. "Dr. Carson, don't tell me you're going to go overboard with your heroic measures and give the damsel in distress the house?"

"I just wanted to say thank you," he explained, his words laced with guilt. "And I think after everything we've been through the past couple of days, you should be calling me John."

Sarah offered him a tired smile. "You're welcome, John."

What am I doing? John thought to himself as Sarah stepped back inside, the warmth of her skin still tingling over his hand. Why couldn't he have denied her offer and let her keep the only home she had ever known? Curse his blasted pride and undying desire to have a house of his own!

His feelings for Sarah were foolish and only temporary. He couldn't care for her. He didn't know how. Never in his adulthood had he ever cared for or loved someone. And no one had ever cared for or loved him.

All he had ever wanted was a house to call his own—a home that no one could ever take away from him. And his dream had finally come true. But what good was a dream if it hurt someone else?

"Stop thinking that way," John said aloud. "I've earned this."

He had worked too hard to create a new life for himself and become a respectable doctor. He wasn't going to risk being hurt again and lose what was rightfully his because of a mystifying woman, no matter how beautiful and charming she might be.

Chapter Four

Sarah couldn't keep herself from smiling as she walked out of the general store, heading toward the schoolhouse with a bag of gumdrops swinging in her hand, gazing at the dirt road that was once again filled with her neighbors and friends. The sound of laughing, merry conversations, and horse hooves stomping through town echoed in the air. Templeton was back to normal.

She greeted each of her neighbors with a wave and a polite hello, happy to see everyone in town smiling as broadly as she was. It was only when she reached her father's clinic and saw Dr. John Carson's name hanging on the sign on the door that her smile faded. Now that life was becoming routine again, she had no choice but to face her uncertain future.

"It's really his clinic now," Sarah whispered and gently ran her fingertips over the newly carved letters.

With a sigh, she stepped away from the sign and stared into the clinic through the dusty window. Her eyes darted around the room, searching for her father's memorable items hidden beneath the numerous boxes of medical supplies waiting to be unpacked.

"Howdy, Sarah!" a familiar twang called out suddenly, and Pap Dickens' round face appeared in the window.

"Good heavens!" Sarah gasped, dropping the gumdrops to the ground. "You startled me, Pap."

Pap quickly opened the door and stepped outside. "I didn't mean to scare ya, hon. I'm mighty sorry."

"Oh, it's all right," Sarah assured the kind old man and dusted off the bag of candy. "No harm done, May's gumdrops are still perfectly intact. Besides, I needed to stop daydreaming anyway."

"Little daydreamin' might do ya good. Must be hard comin' into town for the first time in weeks, seein' that new sign and all," Pap figured. "It was hard enough for me to put it up. I didn't even wanna make the darned thing, but Betty North insisted that the new doc needed a sign of his own. So she wrote the letters out fer me and I carved 'em out."

Sarah smiled at Pap Dickens' loyalty to her father and his constant kindness toward Mrs. North. "The two of you created a beautiful sign together, just as nice as the one my father had. Thank you for doing it, Pap. John's the doctor now and he deserves to have his name on the door. It'll probably be a nice surprise after working at a hospital so long and never having one of his own."

"Well, I guess," Pap grumbled, kicking at the dirt with his boot. "But if you'd just step inside fer a minute, I got somethin' fer ya."

"I suppose May can wait an extra minute or two for her gumdrops," Sarah said and followed her old friend into the clinic.

She took a deep breath when she stepped inside, comforted by the smell of peppermint that still hung in the air. Her father had always said he kept his clinic filled with jars of the sweet candy to make visits easier for his youngest patients, but she had always known he ordered it monthly from the general store because it was her favorite.

"Now, I know I got it around here somewheres," Pap mumbled as he searched the examining room. "Aha!" he cried out triumphantly after looking under a folded sheet. "Here we go. Thought you might like to keep this."

For a moment, Sarah stood wordlessly. Tears glistened in her eyes when she saw the aged wooden sign in Pap's hands bearing her father's name: Gene Bethel. Gingerly, she took it from him and hugged it to her chest.

"Oh, Pap, thank you so much. That was very kind of you."

"Ah, don't get all teary-eyed. I just didn't have much use for it. Since I can't—"

"Read writin', can't write readin'," Sarah interjected.

"Well, I'll be," Pap said, taking off his straw hat and scratching his balding head. "Have I said that before?"

"Only once or twice," Sarah told him with a wink. "There's so much stuff in here," she commented, looking at all the boxes and bags spread over the floor and piled on top of counters. "No wonder you had a hard time finding the sign. I can't believe John has so many things to keep in the clinic. I might not be able to store my belongings here after all."

"You know how city folks is, always havin' things they don't need. Boy's got more clothes than the whole town put together shoved in here."

"Clothes?" Sarah repeated with a suspicious arch of her brow. "What are his clothes doing here? He told me you took all of his belongings out to the house right after I gave it to him willingly. I thought you and Mrs. North had been packing my things and unloading his while he and I were helping the last remaining scarlet fever patients at the schoolhouse."

"Well . . . You see . . . We meant to, but things just didn't work out, that's all," he stammered.

"Pap," Sarah said, sounding like she was about to lecture a naughty child, "what did you do?"

Pap heaved a sigh and peered up at her sheepishly. "I didn't do nothin' bad. I just figured that it would be best to keep the doc's stuff here in case he decided to be a real man and let you keep your pa's house. It just ain't right for him to be livin' there."

"It's fair," Sarah insisted. "He had a contract and I told him he could have the home without any complaining from me. I thought it was the least I could do considering how much he did for all of us."

"That's what doctors is 'spose to do, anyway," Pap mumbled, crossing his scrawny arms. "A real man would stay at the clinic and let you keep that home. You know, if you wanted me to, I could get a group of fellers to talk to that young city slicker and tell him how men out here treat ladies."

"No, you won't," she ordered. "I know very well there would be punches thrown instead of words and there isn't any need for that."

"Oh, fine," he relented with a grunt, "so maybe it weren't the best thing to do. But at least now you have time to get your things together on your own. Betty said it wasn't proper for her to be loadin' up your stuff. She didn't want to forget anything that might be important to ya with your ma and pa gone. The doc can give you a few days to gather your things and have a little time left in the house you growed up in. It'd be good for you to sleep somewhere other than the schoolhouse for a couple of nights before you move into your new home."

"I'm not sure you could call this a home," Sarah whispered as she looked through the clinic. "But it will have to do for now."

"I still say—"

"I know, Pap," she interrupted and planted a kiss on his cheek. "You think the house should be mine. But we both know it wasn't built for the town doctor's daughter; we might as well get used to it. But thank you for thinking of me. I'm looking forward to spending some extra time at home before Dr. Carson moves in. But now I really need to get back to May."

"I'll get used to it," Pap muttered as he tugged his straw hat over his eyes, "but I don't have to like it. When you get back, tell the doc I'll be over soon to get the rest of his things."

Sarah opened the door and stepped outside. "I will. And thank you again for everything you've done for me, even the devious things."

When she returned to the dirt road, Sarah stared up ahead at the schoolhouse. She had savored every moment of her walk to the general store—after weeks of treating sick towns-people, the schoolhouse had begun to feel like a prison. But now as she looked at it from the outside, she began to see the beauty in the old building again: the white paint glowing in the sunlight, the steeple rooftop, and the cross on the door. While she had been praying faithfully, she had nearly forgotten the schoolhouse doubled as a church.

A smile crept over her lips when she climbed up the steps and walked through the door, thankful that Reverend Harrin's life had been spared during the epidemic and pleased to know that tomorrow morning, her neighbors would be filling the pews to hear his Sunday morning service.

"So ya finally decided to come back?" May asked as Sarah entered, looking over her shoulder at the doorway. "I was afraid ya left town with my gumdrops, Ned would never show up to take me home, and I'd be stuck here lonely and hungry forever! I can't believe I'm the last person to get to leave after being . . . being . . . What's that big word?"

Sarah laughed and sat down in the pew beside her best friend. "You were quarantined. Now, stop panicking; you'll be back at home soon. We both know Ned Gibson would never forget about you. And I'm glad to see your appetite is back, May Taylor."

"Soon to be May Gibson," May corrected excitedly.

"Excuse me, Mrs. Gibson," Sarah apologized, handing over the gumdrops while her eyes scanned the empty room. "Where did John go?"

May popped a handful of candy into her mouth. "He got really hot packin' up the last of his things and went out back to the water pump to cool himself off. Why do you care?"

"I don't care," Sarah replied briskly. "I just needed to give him a message from Pap, that's all."

"I bet," May joked. "I'm taken by Ned and even I was sad the doc went outside."

"What are you talking about?"

"As if you don't know, Sarah. Dr. Carson is one of the most handsome men in Templeton. And don't you go tellin' Ned I said that, either!"

Sarah shrugged. "I hadn't noticed."

"Do you really expect me to believe ya? It may have taken me a little while to notice because I had been so sick, but now I'm seein' clearly."

"Seeing what?"

"That the new doctor may be the perfect match for you."

"What?" Sarah gasped. "May, you must be delirious again. Really, I don't want to hear another of your lectures about me finding a husband."

May sighed and rolled her eyes. "I didn't say you should grab him and get hitched. I just think there may finally be a man here in Templeton worthy of you."

"Worthy? I've never considered myself too good for anyone in town. We both know very well why I was never courted. I wasn't like you and the rest of the girls. While you were all learning practical skills from your mothers and socializing with the other kids, I was with my father helping people. None of the boys ever saw me as a potential wife.

Who wants a wife who can help heal illnesses or injuries but can't even cook or knit?"

The words stung as Sarah said them. All of her life, she had known she was different from the other girls in Templeton, but inside she was the same. She longed to have a husband and start a family of her own.

May shook her head. "Oh, Sarah, don't say things like that! Most boys were just scared of your pretty face, book smarts, and quick temper. But Dr. Carson's different. You have more in common."

"We most certainly do not!" Sarah argued. "He's a fine doctor, I'll give him that, but he's also arrogant and materialistic. Do you think I am too?"

"No, not at all. But he's smart and alone here, just like you. Why live a lonely life when you might have a chance at somethin' better?"

Sarah smiled weakly. "Is that what this is *really* about? You don't want me to be alone?"

May stared down at the floor. "Sort of. Ned and me are gonna be hitched just as soon as I've got all my energy back and the harvestin' is over. But he said if you don't have a place to stay figured out soon, you'd be welcome to stay with us. But I know you and I know you won't accept the offer."

"You're right," Sarah clarified. "I won't. I'm not getting in the way of two newly married lovebirds. Besides, everyone's getting too upset about this. It's not like I'm leaving town right now. I'll just be staying at the clinic instead of my old house. You remember the nice bedroom that's upstairs, don't you? You stayed there when you hurt your leg a few years ago."

"I remember, but you helped save this town and should have better than an old bedroom in a clinic. And you don't even know how long you're gonna have that! Maybe I should give in and let Ned convince the doctor to give up the house his way."

"No. I don't want Pap, Ned, or anyone else giving John a hard time over this. It was his medical knowledge that saved lives, not mine."

"You make excuses for the snobby doctor?" May challenged.

"No, I just don't think he should be mistreated because of my situation. It's not his fault my father died."

"Yours either," May echoed, squeezing Sarah's hand. "How can you be so brave? If I were you, I'd be shakin' in my boots."

"I don't have time to be scared," Sarah said with false confidence. "I have packing to do and a letter to write."

"Letter? Who to?" May asked.

"My uncle."

"You have an uncle? I didn't know that."

"He and my father weren't very close and basically lost contact once Papa left Boston," Sarah explained casually. "They were never estranged or bitter, they just had different personalities. Papa wanted a family and a simple life, and my uncle liked being an aristocrat. Maybe he'll be able to help me."

"What if he wants you to move out there?" May panicked. "We could end up just like them and stop bein' friends. I'll be a normal wife out here and you'll be out East livin' with rich folks."

"Don't be silly. He'll probably just send a letter with his condolences. And now, I'm officially done talking about sad things. You have a wedding coming up, and as your maid of honor, I think I should give you a special present."

May smirked. "You're going to quit denying you like Dr. Carson?"

"Think again," Sarah retorted frankly. "I've been thinking about all the things in the house I need to pack up, and it would really be a shame to just tuck away my mother's wedding dress to collect dust. So, I was wondering if you might like to have it?"

"Sarah, I can't take your ma's wedding dress! It won't be as special on your wedding day if I've worn it."

"May, we both know I will never wear it," Sarah whispered, forcing herself to say the words. "Don't look so guilty. I'm offering it to you."

"Thank you, but I just can't take it. It's mighty pretty, but I wouldn't feel right. And you're wrong. One day you're gonna wear it."

Sarah shook her head. "Well, I can tell you really are doing better—you're as stubborn as ever. You don't have to take my mother's wedding dress, but I would like you to come over and look at all the dresses she had. There are some beautiful white ones you could consider. She was taller than you, so your mother may need to make some alterations, but I'm sure we could make it work."

"Thank you," May murmured, overwhelmed. "I just don't know what to say. Your ma had so many pretty dresses that your pa got her from Boston, I'm gonna feel like a princess wearin' one of them! I'm lucky to have a friend like you. Not many girls would share somethin' so special."

"That's because I'm not materialistic or arrogant," Sarah replied as she hugged May. "Unlike *someone else* around here."

"All right, all right," May mumbled defensively. "I won't ever say you've got anything in common with Dr. Carson, even if it is true."

"Will you ever stop?" Sarah asked in mock frustration, unable to fight off a chuckle.

The laughter was contagious as May joined in, filtering through the old schoolhouse so loudly that the giggling young women never heard Ned Gibson enter.

"May, are you causing trouble again?" his deep, gruff tone echoed over their voices.

May quickly tossed aside her gumdrops and ran into his waiting arms. "Oh, Ned! I've missed you so much!"

"I've missed you too," Ned said as he lifted his fiancée into the air. "I'm so glad you can finally go home."

Sarah sat quietly in the pew, not wanting to disturb the happy couple. She couldn't help but smile as she watched Ned's tough, masculine exterior melt away when he hugged May to his chest. He suddenly looked more like an excited little boy than a hardworking farmer.

"Oh, hi, Sarah," Ned greeted her sheepishly when he looked over the brim of his hat and saw her staring up at them. "Didn't mean to get all worked up and forget about ya," he apologized and returned May to the ground.

Sarah stood and joined them. "It's all right. You both looked so happy, I wasn't about to make a sound and ruin it. I'm glad I've got a chance to see you, though, Ned. I was never able to speak with you during your visits with May because Dr. Carson and I were always so busy. I just wanted to thank you for looking after Thunder and my house . . . I mean, John's house."

"Ain't no trouble," Ned retorted as he removed his hat to reveal his unruly red curls. "That darned horse of yours wasn't too happy about me bein' there, though. I swear Thunder is one of the nastiest horses I ever seen. Every time I'd try to feed him I thought he was gonna snap at me."

"I guess he does tend to play favorites," Sarah admitted.

Ned smiled smugly. "I sure can't wait to see the new doc try to handle him. You don't have to be no smart man to know that city boy and Thunder ain't gonna get along."

"Ned," May lectured, "you shouldn't talk about Dr. Carson like that. Sarah doesn't like it when people speak bad about him."

"Why's that?"

"Because she likes him," May announced happily.

"May, I do not like him!" Sarah exclaimed, placing her hands on her hips. "I really don't understand why you keep thinking that. I explained that I just don't want him treated badly on my account. It isn't right."

"Well, speaking of Dr. Carson," Ned grumbled, "my pa and I think he should come to our barn dance. Of course, it won't be for another week or so 'cause of harvestin' gettin' behind schedule, but we'll still have it. I think it's a waste of time to even ask that easterner, but I am thankful to him for savin' May's life and helpin' us all. Givin' him an invite is polite. I was wonderin' if you might ask him, Sarah?"

"Me?" Sarah asked, raising her brow. "Why me? It's your family's celebration, not mine."

"Because you two should go together," May intervened. "Wouldn't that be great, Ned? They could be the guests of honor. Dr. Carson shouldn't get all the credit anyway. Sarah helped just as much as he did, maybe more."

"Oh, May, don't try to make Sarah go with him. Maybe she don't wanna have to spend the night on his arm, listenin' to his complainin'."

"Thank you, Ned," Sarah told him appreciatively, lucky to have Ned nearby to put an end to May's matchmaking schemes.

"Although, it might be for the best," Ned admitted. "Sarah, if you were there, it might keep little girls from gettin' all lovey dovey and buggin' him all night. I hear the talk that's going through town; it seems a man from back East is a catch. And I'd personally be thankful if you were there to put the doc in his place before me or any of the men in town had the chance. Everybody's real thankful to him for what he did, but a lot of folks ain't as nice as Pap and won't put up with him bad-mouthin' our lives."

"Ned, don't jump to conclusions. You don't know that he'll say anything demeaning. You'd probably be upset too, if you left here and had to adjust to a totally different lifestyle. Maybe he doesn't like our town yet, but he obviously cared about our people from the moment he came here or he wouldn't have tried so hard to save us."

"And the excuses keep coming," May said suspiciously. "Still certain ya don't like him?"

"Well, I don't *dis*like him," Sarah clarified. "I just respect him. And I hope everyone else will as well. I've been so isolated, I wasn't aware that he was developing a poor reputation or that girls were becoming interested in learning more about him," she added, feeling an unwanted twinge of jealousy.

"Young gals are just gettin' excited 'cause they've never met a city feller before," Ned mumbled, rolling his green eyes. "Dumbest thing I ever seen."

"It is dumb," May agreed as she linked her arm through his. "Besides, all the girls in town actin' like gossips are far too young to be with Dr. Carson, anyway. They're still children and need to be learnin' instead of courtin'. The only woman left in town that might even be right for him is Sarah."

As soon as she finished speaking, May's cheeks flushed with color. "Oh, Sarah, I didn't mean for it to sound like that! I mean, it's not like you're an old maid. It's just that all the girls our age are already hitched or matched up. And—"

"May," Sarah interjected calmly, "it's okay. I know you didn't mean it as an insult."

"Good," May breathed in relief.

"We shouldn't even worry about it," Ned commented dryly. "I doubt this doc will want to go to a barn dance. He probably thinks we dance on pig droppings."

Sarah bit down on her lip, fighting away a smile as she remembered John's foolish worries. "Well, I promise I'll tell him he's officially invited. And you know I wouldn't miss it, but I don't think Dr. Carson and I will be making a grand entrance together. Maybe if he's the center of attention and getting gazed at by young, lovesick girls, he'll start liking Templeton better."

"I guess I can settle for that answer," May relented.

"I'm glad," Sarah replied, "but we really shouldn't keep chattering away. You should go back home and get some rest. Your parents are probably going mad waiting for you. I'm sure they want to spend as much time with you as possible before you become a married lady."

"Sarah's right," Ned seconded, speaking firmly. "We just got the town back to normal, we don't want things goin' backwards."

"I know better than to argue with you two," May grumbled. "Just let me get my gumdrops."

"I'll get them," Sarah offered. "You should let Ned take you out to the wagon and get you settled."

"All right. Just don't sneak any of my candy."

"I promise," Sarah assured her with a laugh as she walked back to the pew.

Quickly, she scooped the bag of gumdrops into her hand and hurried out of the schoolhouse. As she stepped onto the grass and felt the cool fall wind blowing through her hair, she suddenly stood frozen and watched Ned and May wistfully.

Ned walked beside May slowly, not wanting to rush her. When they reached his wagon, he gently placed his hands on her waist and lifted her up into the seat. Sarah released a dreamy sigh while Ned tucked May under a blanket, and found herself wishing she had someone to love her so unconditionally and not be afraid to show it. She shut her eyes as she daydreamed, surprised when an image of John Carson flashed across her mind and her cheek warmed from the memory of his hand resting there a few days ago.

"Sarah!" May called.

Sarah's eyes flew open when she heard her name. "Oh, sorry, May," she mumbled as she handed her the sack. "My mind was wandering. You have a safe trip and stay warm."

May leaned over carefully and hugged her. "I will. Thank you so much. I don't know if I'll ever be able to repay you."

"Seeing you better is all the thanks I need."

"Giddyap!" Ned hollered to his horse as he pulled on the reins. "See ya at church tomorrow, Sarah!"

Sarah waved to her friends as their wagon headed off toward the outskirts of Templeton. She took in a deep breath and wondered why she had found herself daydreaming of a romantic courtship and why John's face had entered her mind. She had never been prone to daydreaming while others were around and had always prided herself for her calm and serious nature. But now, she couldn't seem to keep childish fairy-tale fantasies from invading her thoughts.

She recalled May's insistence that she and John attend the annual barn dance together, and the jealousy that plagued her as she heard of the young girls in town being fascinated by the doctor.

Over the previous weeks, while she and John had worked diligently together to ensure that the scarlet fever outbreak would come to a permanent end, he had begun to appreciate her help and even started showing her new techniques and medical literature. She had believed she was beginning to see beyond his cold exterior. His touch was always soft as their fingertips brushed together when they traded off medical instruments. And his dark eyes were no longer filled with sadness and anger when he looked at her, but with a gentle glow.

Sighing, Sarah remembered how Ned had ignored Dr. Carson and grew possessively protective of May when he had brought her to the schoolhouse after she had taken ill. He had seen the difference between himself and John from the start. The sophisticated clothing, clean-shaven face, advanced vocabulary and mannerisms. Naturally, all the unmarried women in town would be intrigued by John Carson.

Yet, it seemed so unfair. She was different from many of the other women in Templeton. Her father had filled her mind with knowledge, trained her to assist him, and fulfilled her mother's wish that she be raised as a lady. But an educated woman with a spectacular vocabulary and medical skills wasn't viewed as unique and attractive by men. And John Carson, even if he had told her she was pretty, was not an exception.

Suddenly, Sarah understood why he had wanted her home so desperately. He didn't have a family or friends in Boston, and he had come to Missouri to start a new life for himself. Maybe he didn't want the house for only himself, but for a wife and family of his own someday. And if he had accepted the house from her so easily, he must obviously not have seen her as a potential wife. Once again, someone had overlooked her.

"Pull yourself together," Sarah berated, giving herself a mental shake.

It was foolish to be upset and jealous over a man she wasn't even attracted to. Let someone else deal with his ever-changing personality and defend his regal ways. She had much more important things to deal with than the prospective love life of the new doctor.

Quietly, Sarah stepped back into the schoolhouse, taking in the silence that laced the air. It was mesmerizing to think only weeks ago the small building had been filled with her sick neighbors and friends from wall-to-wall. And now it was empty, and those whose lives had been spared had returned to their homes.

She paced around nervously, annoyed by the echo of her own footsteps. Is this what would become of her? Would she become a lonely woman who spent her days pacing the hours away?

Now that things were taken care of, Dr. Carson wouldn't need her assistance. A grimace surfaced as Sarah recalled his childish remark the day they met: *How am I supposed to depend on you for any assistance? You're probably not even able to read a book on modern medicine, let alone practice it!*

During the epidemic, he had accepted her assistance, but

then, he had been desperate. Now that life was tranquil once again, would he want to toss her aside for a formally trained nurse?

The thought of lodging above the clinic, being so close she could hear the sick patients being treated downstairs, but too far away to provide any help, ate away at her. Never before had she realized that medicine had become such an important part of her life until she feared it might be taken away.

Long ago she had accepted the reality that her dreams of being a wife and mother would never come true, but she refused to walk away from the opportunity to use her medical skills. Just because her father had died didn't mean his dreams for her had to.

"I'll just inform him that I won't quit assisting him. And I'll refuse to take no for an answer! Maybe I could convince him that he would benefit from my help. I could work in exchange for rent. Or I could offer to take care of cleaning the clinic after hours. He probably thinks that's beneath him anyway."

Sarah's sporadic murmuring and scattered thoughts lingered in the air as she marched out of the schoolhouse, preparing to deliver her plan to Dr. Carson. She sighed when she didn't see him at the water pump, worrying her determination would fade if she didn't find him soon. Turning her head, she felt a bit of relief when she saw John resting only a few feet away.

As soon as she reached him, Sarah's dedication subsided. She found herself speechless as she stared at him lying lazily in the grass under a tree with his arm slung over his face to block the bright afternoon sunlight that broke through the bare branches. A smile crept over her lips as she looked at his long body and the outline of muscles hidden beneath the sleeve of his bent arm, and the flecks of gold that appeared in his dark blond hair in the sunlight. May was right. He was handsome—incredibly handsome.

It wasn't just assisting with medicine that she was going to miss. She was going to miss working with *him.* At first she had resented John and loathed his personality, but now she saw more mystery than ego in him. She still hadn't forgotten the night when the miraculous recovery began. He had been worried about her restlessness and wanted her to be healthy. He'd spoken to her kindly and even sat at her side while they welcomed a new morning together. He'd wiped away her tears. And every time she thought of it, her skin tingled at the recollection.

Taking a deep breath, Sarah pushed away the thoughts that threatened to take away her strong will. Perhaps she wanted to solve the mystery behind Dr. Carson, but he didn't want to learn more about her. He hadn't offered to let her keep her home or asked her to continue working for him at the clinic. If she wanted to continue working in the medical field, she was going to have to evade her schoolgirl emotions and re-main focused.

"John!" Sarah said crisply, not concerned if she awoke him from a nap. "I need to talk to you."

"Now isn't a good time," John mumbled back slowly. "Surely it can wait. Just let me rest here."

"No, it cannot wait," Sarah argued. "I want to talk to you about the clinic. I appreciate that you offered to let me stay there free of charge, but I don't believe it's right for me to stay without earning my keep. I'm going to assist you with your patients. You know from experience I'm a good worker, and I could also help with the cleaning. You'll find it's hard to keep the clinic spotless without help."

"Fine," John answered tiredly.

"Fine?" Sarah blurted, completely surprised and relieved when he didn't put up a fight. When had the melancholy Dr. Carson started allowing others to make his decisions for him?

"Yes, you're a good worker, as you said. I'd be lucky to have you around. Now, kindly let me get back to my nap."

Sarah's eyes narrowed in concern as she strained to hear John when his words faded to a whisper. "Are you all right?"

"I'd be perfectly fine if I were allowed to take a simple nap!" John answered hastily and stumbled up onto his feet, keeping one arm draped clumsily over his face.

She followed after him and grasped his loose sleeve. "You are not fine! If you were fine, you'd let me see your face!"

"Very well!" John cried in frustration, spinning around to face her, only to find himself clinging to her shoulders as his head filled with dizziness.

Sarah's blood ran cold when she felt the heat from John's trembling hands spread onto her shoulders. She tilted her head, looking up at his deeply flushed cheeks and the bloodshot, glazed eyes that stared back at her. The fear she thought she had finally forgotten returned at full throttle. "You've got scarlet fever."

Chapter Five

Wearily, Sarah peeled a damp cloth from John's forehead, finding its cool texture had already warmed from his rising temperature. Routinely, she reached over into the bowl, pressing the cloth into the water and back to his brow. For hours, she had been at his bedside, watching over him diligently.

At first he had been able to communicate with her, insisting he could treat himself and protesting when she forced him to ride over to the clinic in Pap's old wagon, complaining at each bump in the road. But he had soon slipped into delirium as his fever rose uncontrollably. And now, Sarah longed to hear his ridiculous complaints and find herself arguing with him again.

She struggled to look at him and see such a robust, vibrant man lying helplessly in bed without remembering her father. The memory of his death still haunted her. He had died in her arms, his mind so altered by the fever, he didn't even know he was being held by his own daughter.

The irony was overwhelming. The second town doctor to

contract scarlet fever. No matter how she tried, Sarah couldn't keep herself from worrying John might lose his life just as her father had. And there would be nothing she could do to stop it.

Turning away from his flushed face, Sarah tiredly pulled herself to her feet and began to pace around the room anxiously. She kept her eyes fixed on a small bottle sitting on top of the dresser beside the water-filled basin. It was full of the mixture of belladonna John had brought with him from Boston. There was a chance his life could be spared. Many others treated with the homeopathic treatment had lived, but Dr. Carson had been presiding over their care and measuring the dosages of their medication. And the slates where he had documented the dosage for each patient had been wiped clean days ago in preparation for the return of school lessons.

Sarah had administered medication countless times, but only after being told what dosage to give. Relentlessly, she had read through passages in his books on homeopathy, but never found a succinct recommendation to help her.

When John let out a painful moan, Sarah ended her pacing and returned to his side. A lump formed in her throat when she pressed her hand to his burning forehead—providing a vivid reminder that she couldn't wait much longer to make a decision, no matter how incapable she felt. She remembered reading and seeing with her own eyes that the people who received medicine immediately were the ones to make the quickest and fullest recoveries.

Staring down at Dr. Carson, seeing his face tensed in pain and hearing his raspy breath, Sarah silently scolded herself. Only hours ago, she had been at the schoolhouse, filled with jealousy and making assumptions about his desire to move into her house. If only she had fought away her silly emotions, she might have gotten to him sooner and been calm enough to ask for assistance measuring the amount of medication he would need before the fever altered his clarity.

Gently, she brushed her fingers across his brow, pushing his hair away from his eyes. Concerned by his fever, she pulled back the blankets layering him and rewet the cloth that been resting on his forehead. In soft strokes, she wiped his warm face, then trailed over his neck. She slid her hand underneath the open buttons on his shirt, spreading the cool water over his flesh. Her heartbeat quickened when her fingertips skimmed over his firm chest.

She retrieved her hand immediately, flustered and surprised by her reaction. Instantly, she thought of May's taunting insistence that Sarah liked him, which she had vehemently negated. Had her best friend been right?

Some of the things May said had been true; she finally did have someone in town who shared her knowledge of medicine and mannerly ways. And after all the chaos they had worked through together, it would be nearly impossible not to develop some sort of friendship.

But when Sarah glanced back at his face and remembered the pangs of jealousy she suffered when she thought of him spending time with another woman in town, she begrudgingly began to wonder if it truly was feelings of friendship she was beginning to feel for him or something more.

"Sarah!" a twang-filled voice hollered from outside, followed by a loud bang on the door. "Sarah!"

Sarah stood, knowing at once the voice belonged to Pap Dickens. She released a sigh, thankful to have a distraction from her own thoughts, but worried to know what could have brought Pap to the clinic at such a late hour. She hurried to the window and was startled by the sunlight pouring into the bedroom when she drew back the curtain. She saw Pap and Mrs. North standing in the street below.

John had already gone an entire night without medication. She simply couldn't keep doubting herself. She had to begin treating him soon if she wanted him to make a full recovery. But if she made a mistake, would he recover at all?

Kneeling over the bed, Sarah squeezed John's hand and whispered into his ear, "I'll be right back," wanting him to know that he wouldn't be left alone and wondering if he could hear her.

She hurried out of the bedroom and down the stairs, worrying Pap's relentless pounding and yelling would wake John and anyone else nearby.

"Good morning," Sarah greeted hurriedly as she pulled the door open. "Please come inside," she urged, shivering against the chill in the morning air. "Are you both all right?"

Pap nodded his head while he escorted Mrs. North inside. "Fine and dandy. Just came by to see how the doc was doin'. When I picked up Betty fer church this mornin' and told her about him, she was set on comin' here with me. And you know how this gal is once she's got her mind set," he said with a complimentary grin. "I knew darn well there was nothin' I could do to talk her out of it."

"That's right," Mrs. North stated frankly. "I got some things together for you," she explained, lifting up a basket. "I told Pap I would not step foot into church until I had brought you some food. You're just like your pa, Sarah Bethel, and I know you'll be payin' so much attention to Dr. Carson, you won't think of takin' care of yourself. I didn't have enough notice to fix anything special, but I brought you the corn muffins left over from breakfast."

"Mrs. North," Sarah whispered as she accepted the basket, "this is wonderful. Thank you very much, but you didn't have to—"

"Oh, fiddlesticks," the old woman interjected. "It's nice to do something for somebody besides sort their mail. Now, how's our young doctor doing? Any better?"

"I'm afraid not," Sarah answered sadly. "His fever has only gone up since he came here. He's delirious now."

"Is that right?" Pap mumbled in surprise and scratched his

chin. "Why, the way that boy was gripin' about my wagon yesterday, I figured he'd be right as rain by mornin'."

Sarah smiled weakly at the memory. "The illness was only beginning then. The worst may be yet to come."

"But you can fix him," Mrs. North insisted. "You and Dr. Carson got lots of folks better."

"I was only helping then," Sarah reminded her.

"You've always helped, Sarah," Mrs. North told her in a motherly tone and patted her cheek. "You're a real smart girl."

Sarah sighed. "Thank you. But I am not as wise as you believe. I am not a doctor, only an assistant. It was John who measured the dosages of belladonna to be administered and prepared them for consumption, not me."

"So that's all you have to figure out, dear, just the dosage?" Mrs. North inquired. "The medicine is already here?"

"Yes."

"You can figure it out," Pap assured her. "You're the smartest gal in these parts, doctor or not! I bet you're even smarter than that city boy thinks he is."

"Pap's right," Mrs. North seconded. "After all, you were the one treatin' everybody before Dr. Carson came here."

"That was different," Sarah persisted. "Then I knew what I was doing."

"You still do, honey. You know which medicine to give him and have it here. All you have to do is figure out how much. Right now, you're so flustered you can't think back to the outbreak and remember things, that's all," Mrs. North proclaimed.

Maybe Mrs. North was right. Throughout her sleepless night, Sarah had wondered if she was becoming as delirious as John. She had tried to clear her mind a dozen times but always failed when her worry took over.

"I am a little frazzled," Sarah admitted reluctantly, having never allowed anyone in town to know how much her father's death and the horrible epidemic had really affected her. "Every time I think back, all I remember is Papa."

Pap offered her a sympathetic grin, revealing the spacious gaps in his teeth. "Well, Gene Bethel was a darned good man, and everybody is missin' him. But it's gotta be harder on you."

"Even if it is," Sarah murmured, "it's not an excuse. In all my life, I've never felt like such a scatterbrain. I wasn't prepared at all for this. I had finally let myself relax again. I was a fool to think another person wouldn't get sick."

"There's a difference between foolish and hopeful," Mrs. North countered. "Now, just calm yourself and think back. You said it was the dosages you were worried about? Well, at the post office, I know we have things to help figure out how much it costs to mail somethin', dependin' on the weight. Surely you've got somethin' around here to help you do the same or a chart in one of those books."

Sarah shook her head. "No, and I looked through his books from cover to cover hoping to find some kind of guide. And the slates we were using in the schoolhouse were already cleaned."

"That was my doin'," Pap grumbled, pulling off his straw hat and wringing it in his hands. "I was an old fool and wiped 'em clean!"

"Pap, you are not an old fool," Sarah promised him. "John told you it was all right to clean them. You were just helping, like you always are. I don't know what I would've done if you hadn't shown up and helped me bring John here."

"Ah, right place, right time, that's all," Pap mumbled.

"Well!" Mrs. North announced, clapping her hands together. "There's only one thing left to do. And that's to put our heads together so we can figure this out and help our young doctor."

"If only I could remember how much medicine John prepared for each person," Sarah wished. "I was always so busy trying to wake everyone, I never paid too much attention."

"Surely you can remember a little," Mrs. North said gently. "Just think back, honey. It will come if you stop worryin' so much and let it."

Sarah took a deep breath and sank into an empty chair, feeling emotionally and physically drained as she struggled to remember vivid details from the epidemic. She shut her eyes and thought back to when she was a little girl and constantly losing her hair ribbons while she got dressed for school in the morning. Calmly, her father would tell her to retrace her actions, starting from when she got out of bed, and his method never failed. If only she were still searching for ribbons.

Silently, Sarah recalled her time spent with John at the schoolhouse, visualizing the order the patients were lying in as they made their rounds to administer the medication. It was the same pattern every day, like clockwork.

First, they would tend to Milly Davis and the other young children who would need the smallest dose. Then they'd move on to May and the rest of the women who had taken ill. And finally, the men: Reverend Harrin, Caleb Patten . . .

"Caleb Patten!" Sarah muttered, feeling a rush of nervous energy. "Caleb Patten," she said once again, lifting her head to face her friends. "Wouldn't you say he's about the same size as John?"

Mrs. North nodded. "Yes, I suppose. Maybe only five or ten pounds difference."

"What's that got to do with anythin', Sarah?" Pap asked curiously, watching as she leapt from her chair and hurried through the clinic, looking through the cabinets haphazardly.

"I think I remember how much of the medicine John gave to Caleb Patten. It was always a struggle for John to wake him and keep him awake long enough to get the medicine down," Sarah explained after she successfully retrieved a spoon.

"Well, what do I do to help?" Pap asked anxiously. "There's

got to be somethin' more we can do besides just give him medicine."

"Should I ask Reverend Harrin to clear the church for you again?" Mrs. North questioned, seeming as desperate to help as Pap.

Sarah shook her head. "No, that isn't necessary yet. For now, it would be best if I treat John here. Hopefully, since I was able to isolate him immediately, no one else will take ill. But I suppose there is always a risk that more people could get sick."

Taking a deep breath, she quickly regained her calm demeanor and natural leadership and prepared a plan. "We need to spread the news through town that if anyone begins to show even the slightest symptoms, they need to be brought to me directly. And I'll need to send word to Boston requesting more belladonna. We only have one bottle left."

"I'll head over to the church and start tellin' people," Pap volunteered. "And you and Betty can figure out what message you need to send from the post office."

"Thank you," Sarah replied. "And you stay bundled up so you don't catch a chill in the morning air."

"Ah, I'm as healthy as a horse!" Pap proclaimed, marching out the door in a dramatic exit.

"He's as healthy as an old horse," Mrs. North mumbled worriedly as she watched Pap climb into his old wagon. "But he's young at heart. Wouldn't you agree, Sarah?" When Sarah didn't answer, the older woman rested a comforting hand on her shoulder. "What's wrong, darlin'?"

Sarah gripped the spoon tightly. "There's only one bottle left. What if that isn't enough to help him? You would think after everything that happened with the epidemic, I would be immune to fear. But I think I'm even more afraid now than I was then."

"What do you mean?"

"John's life is literally resting in my hands. If we don't

have enough or I mess up on the amount, he could die. And I would be to blame."

"Think about what will happen if you do nothing at all," Mrs. North whispered, gently running her hand over Sarah's braided hair. "He'll get better, you'll see."

"Mrs. North, my father had been exposed to illnesses all his life, and even he couldn't survive this."

"You can't lose faith," Mrs. North insisted, keeping a soothing tone. "You're forgettin' you aren't the only one watching over our young doctor."

Sarah turned her head slowly and saw the old woman pointing heavenward.

"Everyone at church this morning is goin' to be sayin' a bushel of prayers to make sure John's name drifts up to the Lord's ears. The Lord will do His job. Now you go do yours."

Sarah squinted in the dim candlelight as she glanced down at the blank piece of paper resting beneath her hands. Many times throughout the day she had sat down at the edge of the dresser, dipped her pen into a jar of ink, and prepared to write her uncle to tell him of her father's passing, but each time she had failed.

It seemed so odd to be writing to a relative whom she had never met and knew very little of. Her stomach churned from the embarrassment of confiding in him about her current situation, worrying he would believe she was contacting him only to ask for money or a place to stay. But truthfully, those were the least of her worries.

Her mind always turned to John. Endless thoughts of dread ran through her mind whenever she gazed at his flushed face or listened to his whispered words of delirious nonsense. Despite the belladonna she had given him, he had not yet begun to show any sign of improvement. In fact, he had only gotten worse as his fever and delirium raged on.

She had struggled to understand the scattered sentences that stumbled out of his lips during his restless sleep, but had begun to recognize a few familiar names and recurring phrases: Mr. and Mrs. Wilder, Dr. Thompson, and constant pleas for help.

Each word was always said with such anger or fear that Sarah longed to learn more about the mysterious thoughts that haunted John during his illness, wondering if they were only delusions brought on by the fever or horrible memories that had returned to life.

Even when John lay in silence, he was never at peace. He thrashed about violently from side to side, whimpering, his face contorted in pain and sadness. Sarah had tried relentlessly to calm him, speaking in soft, soothing tones as she promised him he was safe, and even singing a lullaby she remembered her father singing to her as a child. But he continued to suffer, oblivious to her heartfelt efforts.

Releasing an inward sigh, Sarah laid down her pen, feeling selfish for even thinking of writing her uncle to tell him of her misfortune while John was fighting for his life. Yet she couldn't bear the thought of another sleepless night without any sort of distraction from her own fears.

During the day, it was fairly simple to keep herself upbeat with visits from Pap and Mrs. North. Pap would chatter on about the latest assignment someone in town had asked him to help with, and Mrs. North would fill her stomach and lecture her about the necessity of eating right and keeping herself well while she cared for John.

But when the dark night arrived, her positive attitude seemed to disappear with the sun. The hustle and bustle that she heard outside the clinic of people coming and going through town turned to silence, and reminded her she was alone. That's when the secret worries reappeared.

Over and over, she recalled the frightful days of the scarlet fever outbreak before John Carson arrived, when she and she alone was trying to save so many lives. She could still see the sea of people lying on the schoolhouse floor in misery. The sounds of their coughing and cries still echoed in her ears. And the memory of the awful day when her father transformed from the care-giving doctor to a patient needing care had yet to fade.

Sarah swallowed roughly, still ashamed of herself for some days wanting to turn her back on the others and only care for her ailing father. But she had never given in to the temptation, knowing he would never forgive her when he recovered. In time, being so preoccupied by all of the ill townspeople and the need to find a doctor to travel west had become a blessing and helped her keep a level head. Having so much responsibility never permitted her to dwell on her father's illness. For a while, she had even allowed her mind to become so cluttered, she never realized that her father, like many other suffering people, might die.

Even when he had died in her arms, she had wanted to pretend he was only sleeping. For hours, he had been in terrible pain and left utterly confused by severe delirium. He twitched about with chills, whispering slurred messages as he drifted in and out of a feverish sleep.

Sarah always felt comforted when he would awaken, seeing his eyes slowly open and gaze up at her face. Even though he glanced at her with a blank stare, she always prayed that somehow deep inside, he still knew she was near him. He had always told her that God had kept a part of her mother alive with their similar features. And He had given Sarah her father's blue eyes because they were the only trait he could pass along to a little girl without ruining her beauty.

And when his eyes shut for the last time, Sarah's heart filled with emptiness, knowing she would never again have the mirrored sparkling, sapphire orbs looking back at her. She had bent down, placed a gentle kiss on her father's forehead, and said a hopeful prayer that he was now free of pain and with her mother once again. Then she covered him with a blanket and tended to the rest of the sick, only leaving herself one short moment to grieve her loss.

Wiping a tear from her cheek, Sarah managed to feel grateful as she returned to the present. Even though her father had been severely ill, he had never seemed as distressed and miserable as John Carson. And despite his memory loss, he appeared to be at peace when he passed on.

Sighing, Sarah listened to John's sad pleas growing in volume and turning into anger. Quickly, she pulled herself together and hurried to his bedside to help wake him from the nightmare.

"No, you can't have it!" John cried out desperately, thrashing from side to side. "Let go!" he hollered.

"John, it's only a dream," Sarah assured him, keeping her voice loud and clear. "You're all right. No one's trying to take anything from you. Wake up, John," she pleaded with him, dipping a washcloth under the cool water in the nearby basin. "Please wake up," she begged and dabbed his forehead.

Suddenly, John's eyes flew open, tinted red with a feverish panic.

Sarah arched her brow when she stared into his eyes, surprised by the deep sadness and desperation glowing in his narrow gaze. It was as if the fever had turned John Carson into a complete stranger.

"Don't take it!" he hollered again, his voice raising in pitch and sounding much higher, almost childlike. "It's mine! They can't have it!"

"Shh," Sarah soothed. "No one is going to take anything from you, John. It's just you and me," she told him calmly. "I know things might be confusing for you right now, but it's because you're very sick. But there's no reason to worry and be upset. I'm going to take care of you," she promised.

For a moment, John seemed to relax and his breaths came more slowly.

"That's better. I'm going to get you some more medicine, all right?" she told him and turned toward the dresser.

"No!" John screamed violently, quickly bolting up from the mattress, swinging his arms about erratically as he struggled to stand. "No! You can't leave! If you leave, they'll take it!"

"I'm not leaving or letting anyone take anything," Sarah assured him, trying to grasp his arms and help him back into bed before he worsened his condition. "Just lie down and rest," she ordered gently but firmly, while tucking him under the tangled blankets. "I was just going to get you some medicine," she explained, taking a step away and wrapping her fingers around the bottle.

"No!" John hollered once more, tears glittering in his eyes. "Don't!" he implored, reaching out and grasping her hand.

As John jerked at her fingers, Sarah felt her grip loosen. The water still on her skin from the damp cloth thwarted her attempt to catch the bottle, and it slipped away. She watched helplessly as it fell, crashing and breaking into jagged pieces.

"It's mine!" John continued on, completely oblivious to the loud noise and horrific loss as he hollered. "It's all I have left!"

Tears filled Sarah's eyes and spilled onto her cheeks, though she didn't know whether they came from the pain of seeing John transformed into a distraught child or the fear of watching the last of the needed medicine spread in useless puddles across the floor.

Swallowing roughly, she returned her attention to John, even though all of her hope had disappeared with the wasted medicine. He lay on his side shivering, his knees drawn to his chest. Sarah listened closely as she straightened his blankets and heard a meek whisper.

"Please, please don't let them take it," he muttered. "It's all I have left. . . ."

She sat quietly at his bedside and watched a single tear drip down his cheek, completely bewildered by the sight. The arrogant doctor had been replaced by a heartbroken little boy. In her entire life, she had never seen someone so troubled and delirious from a fever. Her desire to learn more about the secrets Dr. Carson carried inside of him intensified, now urged by deep concern instead of curiosity, and a wish to know what he desperately wanted her to protect. What memory could be so painful it turned such a sophisticated man into a panicked child?

Looking at the tortured doctor lying helplessly in bed, Sarah began to fear John's life might come to an end before he had time to heal his painful past and create a promising future.

Now it wasn't the letter to her uncle that she had to write that worried her, but the thought of writing a letter to let the staff at Saint Francis Hospital know that Dr. John Carson had passed away, leaving Templeton without a doctor once again.

Gently, she brushed her hand over his warm cheek, feeling the wet tear spread over her fingertips. "You have to get better, John. This town needs you. *I* need you."

Lifting the cloth from the basin, Sarah knelt down to the floor and began sopping up the puddles. She stopped when she brushed her hand against one of the jagged pieces of glass, not even flinching when it pierced her skin. Helplessly, she stared at the broken bottle, knowing it was just another of the many things she could not fix.

Chapter Six

Rain dripped slowly down the windowpane as Sarah sat perfectly still, watching one raindrop fall after the other. It seemed the perfect accompaniment to the dreary days she had spent at the clinic, unable to end John's raging illness.

She blinked suddenly when Mrs. North appeared in the window, waving to her. Offering the old woman a weak smile, Sarah stood and hurried to the door.

"Come in," she said, ushering her friend inside. "Mrs. North, what are you doing here? You shouldn't be out in this weather."

"Oh, it doesn't matter whether it's rainy or sunny, you still need to eat and have a little company to keep your spirits up," Mrs. North chattered. "Pap's tellin' tall tales at the general store, so I figured I'd stop in here and say hello. Now, I hope this will be enough food," she rambled and placed a basket on the table. "I brought you some bread, a piece of apple pie I had to hide from Pap, and some soup, just in case Dr. Carson was feeling up to eating today."

"That was very kind of you, Mrs. North," Sarah told her gratefully, "but I'm afraid he isn't any better."

"I was worried you'd say that. Such a pity, he's such a young man," Mrs. North lamented with a sigh. "But how about you? You look worn to the bone. I bet you haven't even had time to write that letter you wanted me to send out to New York for ya."

"No, I was too flustered to complete the letter to my uncle. But that doesn't matter. I don't plan on sending it until I am certain of what will happen with John. Right now, he's my main priority."

"Well, what about a letter to go to the hospital in Boston? I thought you had said you were thinkin' about sendin' word to them about John's poor health."

"I never wrote it," Sarah confessed, swallowing roughly. "I feel like if I wrote to them, letting them know how horribly ill John is and that I'll be needing another doctor, I'd be sentencing him to death and giving up hope that he could get better."

"Ah, Sarah, don't worry. We don't have to send a letter. God forbid John doesn't get well, I can have Pap drive me out to Saint Louis. They got one of those telegram machines that I don't think my old hands could ever work. We won't lose hope for our young doctor just yet."

"I feel like I've already given up on him. I barely even stay in the room with him now. It seems nothing I do comforts him or eases the pain, and I already gave him the last of the medicine. I get so tired and frustrated seeing him fade away more and more every day. Every time I force myself to finally open the door and go inside, I'm always afraid he'll be gone."

"I know it must be an awful scary thing, but if you don't go check on him and see how he's doing, you'll never know if he gets better. It sure would be sad to be sick for so long and not have a face to wake up to, don't ya think?"

"Yes, I guess it would," Sarah agreed.

"I reckon it would be especially nice to wake up to a face as pretty as yours, darlin'," Mrs. North added with a sly grin.

"Oh, Mrs. North, not you too!" Sarah groaned, shaking her head. "You're as bad as May."

"I'm not bad at all," the old woman argued. "I just still have my eyes, even if they are fadin' on me. Anybody could see how handsome Dr. Carson is and what a pretty girl you are."

"Ah, Betty!" Pap Dickens' voice echoed into the clinic as he opened the door and stomped inside. "Don't you go fillin' Sarah's head with ideas of needin' to be on the arm of the city feller. Sarah could do better, probably even get herself a real prince. No need to be pairin' her off with some young whippersnapper that don't even know how to treat a lady proper."

"Pap, he's not that bad," Sarah insisted. "And if he doesn't start getting better, you won't have to worry about his behavior much longer."

"Aw, now I sound like a grouchy, mean old man," Pap grumbled. "Just 'cause he's a city feller without manners don't mean I don't wanna see him get better."

"No one would ever associate mean or grouchy with your name, Pap Dickens," Sarah said and wrapped him in a warm hug.

"Gosh, no need to go on like that all day. We need to be gettin' back home before the sun drops and the cold air gets even colder. You ready to get goin', Betty?"

Mrs. North pulled her shawl tightly around her shoulders and nodded. "Yes. Goodbye, Sarah, you take care now, darlin'."

"I will," Sarah promised as she walked the elderly couple to the door. "You two be careful out there."

Sarah glanced out the window, smiling while she watched them walk to Pap's old wagon. It seemed ironic for Betty

North of all people to be prodding someone about their romantic feelings when she would never confess to how she truly felt about Pap.

Sighing, Sarah started up the stairs, knowing she would never confess her sudden feelings for John, either. After all, she was still struggling to understand how she could care so much about him in the first place.

When she came to the top of the staircase, she stood frozen and gazed at the closed door. Something as simple as turning a doorknob suddenly seemed so complicated. Would she find him still suffering from his illness? Or would he have finally taken a turn for the better?

Taking a deep breath, Sarah gained control of her thoughts before she allowed herself to think the worst. She reached out to the knob with a shaking hand and prayed silently as she opened the door. She stepped inside slowly, thankful not to see John tossing and turning restlessly or muttering nonsense in his sleep.

She walked over to the bed and sat down gently on the edge of the mattress, comforted by the sound of his even, deep breaths. Then she squinted and studied his face.

Even though his skin was still dreadfully pale, he looked a little better. His face was no longer tense and filled with frustration. He finally seemed to be calm.

For a moment, Sarah felt a brief sense of excitement and started to wonder if he had finally begun to get better. But it quickly ended when she remembered the other patients who had died during the epidemic who had been so calm and peaceful before they passed on, including her own father.

She lifted her hand but paused before touching his brow. Suddenly, her feelings for John seemed to multiply, along with her desperate hope for him to live.

It wasn't fair. He obviously had suffered horribly before he came to Templeton, and he deserved a chance to start a new life. And it was a life she wanted to be a part of.

Nervously, she stretched her hand across his forehead. His skin was cool and clammy. Sarah's breath caught in her throat and a smile began to tug at the corners of her lips. She left her palm on his brow a few moments longer, wanting to make sure his fever truly had broken and she wasn't dreaming.

Sarah felt tears mist her eyes as she squeezed John's hand and kissed his palm. "I knew not to give up on you, John Carson," she whispered, pressing his hand to her cheek. "I just hope you won't give up on yourself."

Turning her head, she glanced out the window at the sunlight that began to break through the rainy sky. She watched the sunlight spread and felt it strengthen her hope that all of the dark days she and John had suffered through were finally over.

John Carson blinked several times and struggled to force his eyes to stay open. He tried again and again, feeling as though he had been asleep for so long that being awake was a chore. His vision began as a blur at first, then gradually returned to normal. He gazed around the room, trying to figure out where he was and how he had gotten there.

For a moment, the bedroom reminded him of his room in the boardinghouse in Boston: plain and practically empty, with only a single bed, chair, and dresser. But even with the lack of decorations and furniture, there was a feeling of comfort within the four walls that was pleasantly unfamiliar. He listened closely, only to hear birds chirping outside and the echo of a church hymn being sung off in the distance, instead of his rowdy Boston neighbors, and knew he must be in Templeton.

Slowly, he tried to sit up, surprised by how weak and sore his body was. What on earth had happened? Drawing all the strength he could find, he shoved his palms down against the mattress and pushed himself up with trembling limbs.

He rested back against the pillows, lifting his head to see Sarah in the corner of the room, seated by the window, sleeping.

Her long blond hair fell over her shoulder, blocking her face from sight, only allowing him to see her shoulders lift slightly up and down with each deep breath she quietly drew in. She seemed so peaceful John could barely bring himself to distract her, and hated to admit that he would be content to sit silently just watching her.

"Sarah?" John whispered when curiosity got the best of him, his voice plagued by raspy fatigue. "Sarah?"

Sarah raised her head, causing her honey-colored locks to fall back and uncover her face. Slowly, she raised her hands and rubbed her eyes. "Good morning, John," she greeted him with a tired smile. "Welcome back."

"Back?" he inquired.

"You've been ill for days with scarlet fever and quite delirious," Sarah explained as she stood. "Your fever broke yesterday, but I was beginning to wonder if you would ever wake up. How are you feeling?"

"Tired," John mumbled in reply, searching his mind for any memory of what had occurred in the slipped time, only to come up empty-handed. "I had scarlet fever?"

Sarah nodded and sat down at the end of the bed. "Yes, quite a severe case, in fact. You gave everyone quite a scare."

"Everyone?" John chuckled weakly. "The people here barely know me."

"Why does that matter? You helped save this town from being wiped out—of course people care. They wouldn't be in the church right now, praying for you if they didn't."

"That's why people are singing?" he muttered. "I just thought it must be Sunday."

"It's not," Sarah informed him. "And you'll learn quickly that life is different here in Templeton. People truly care for their neighbors. People are more than happy to make you a part of their lives, and to be a part of your new life, if you'll let them."

John rested silently, surprised and honored by the support that the people in Templeton had offered. They had only known him as the town doctor, yet that was enough to invite him into their prayers.

He couldn't help but wonder what had happened during his illness. Why would Sarah be so eager to assure him that the townspeople cared, that he wasn't alone? Had she somehow learned some of the secrets he had wanted to bury forever? Her comments were too heartfelt to be coincidental.

"Do you need anything?" Sarah questioned, interrupting his thoughts. "You haven't eaten in days. Are you hungry?"

"No, not just yet," John responded. "I'm still struggling to get my bearings, but I'm assuming you've been the one taking care of me?"

Sarah smiled. "Yes, even though it might please you to know, at first you insisted quite strongly that you didn't need my help. And you were very unhappy when Pap brought you over here in his wagon."

"Well," John whispered, "that does sound like something that's easy to imagine. I'm very thankful that is one adventure in Pap's wagon I won't have nightmares about."

"You might not," Sarah replied and giggled, "but I'm not so sure about Pap."

John laughed softly with her, feeling a few dry coughs slip through his lips. "I'll have to apologize to him."

"There will be plenty of time for that," Sarah assured him, standing and walking toward the dresser. "Right now, you just need to worry about getting better. You should take a few sips of water while you're sitting up. It might help with that dry cough."

John turned his head slowly, finding even simple movements to be a heavy burden on his tired body. He gazed at Sarah as she lifted the pitcher and poured water into a tiny cup, amazed by the beauty and grace with which she performed even mundane tasks. He squinted when he noticed the bandage wrapped around her hand.

"What happened?" he pondered, trembling as he gestured to her palm.

"Oh, that?" Sarah replied with brief hesitation. "Well, it's just a little scrape from a clumsy accident. Here." She handed him the cup and the worry in her blue eyes evaporated. "Take a few sips before you start coughing again. But little sips—your throat is probably still very tender."

"Thank you," John told her appreciatively, carefully wrapping his hands around the cup. Unsuccessfully, he attempted to raise the cup to his lips, but found himself shaking too badly to keep a steady hold.

Sarah placed her hands over his. "Let me help you."

John smiled at her touch, feeling warmth spread over his fingertips. Gently, she guided the cup to his lips, patiently helping him take a couple of drinks.

"Better?" she asked after he swallowed.

"Much," John answered. "Thank you."

He nestled back into his pillows, unable to break his gaze from Sarah as she set the cup back down. She was certainly a sight for sore eyes and a beautiful vision to wake up to. Yet, there was something different about her, something that he couldn't figure out.

But so much was different now. Only weeks ago, he wouldn't have had a life worth saving. He had been living a daily routine in Boston, tending to his patients by day and sitting alone in the boardinghouse at night, allowing his dark past to control him.

Now he would have the opportunity to see the world with new eyes. He had come to Templeton hating the country landscape, annoyed by his overly friendly and curious neighbors. And the very people he had ignored were the ones who were kind and sincere. For the first time in countless years, he was in a place where people knew his name and his face and cared about him. Somehow knowing that Sarah was one of them made it all mean even more.

"John, are you all right?" Sarah asked worriedly as she glanced into his face. "You look a little dazed."

"Oh, just thinking," John mumbled sheepishly.

"Why don't you try to go back to sleep?" she suggested and adjusted the bed covers. "You'll still need to stay in bed for a few days. There won't be much else for you to do besides think."

"I guess you're right," John agreed. "And Sarah . . ." he whispered and reached out weakly to rest his hand over hers. "I wanted to say thank you. Thank you for taking care of me, for making me well. I know it couldn't have been easy."

Sarah stood silently a moment and stared down at their joined hands. "You don't have to thank me," she muttered, giving his fingers a light squeeze before slowly letting go to draw the curtains. "That's what my father raised me to do, no matter what the circumstances were. Sleep well."

John shut his eyes, gradually letting sleep overtake him, smiling when he finally realized what had been different about Sarah. Her long blond hair that she had always kept in a braid flowed freely over her shoulders and perfectly framed her heart-shaped face.

Clinging to the banister, John slowly made his way down the stairs, pausing when his footsteps became shaky and weak. He smiled when he looked in the examining room and saw Sarah rummaging through a cabinet full of medical supplies.

"Good afternoon," he greeted quietly.

"John, I didn't know you had gotten out of bed," Sarah said as she looked over her shoulder. "Were you getting hungry? Mrs. North just dropped off some food and I was going to take you a tray as soon as I was finished here."

"Well, I must admit I am quite hungry, but it wasn't my reason for getting out of bed. After three days, I simply couldn't take any more bed rest and needed to be back on my feet again. I thought I would come down here for a while and get a feel for the clinic."

"I'm glad you're feeling better," Sarah replied, tossing aside a bandage. "Let me help you the rest of the way down."

"Taking inventory?" John assumed. He gripped her outstretched hands, thankful for the extra support and her comforting touch.

"No, I was just going to change the bandage on my hand, but I'd be happy to get you some lunch first. Mrs. North's homemade bread is a real treat. You should be well enough to eat something other than soup now."

"I'm sure her bread is delicious, but it can wait. Let me help you. I haven't been able to treat a patient in ages and I am getting a little eager to."

"A mild scrape hardly qualifies someone as a patient."

"Humor a recovering man; it will only take a few minutes," John insisted.

Sarah rolled her eyes playfully and boosted herself onto the examining table. "Fine, go ahead and look. I don't doubt you're eager to be in charge again."

John smiled at her candor as he took her hand in his, untied the bandage, and gently peeled it away from her skin. His eyes widened when he saw the jagged red line etched over her palm. "I thought you said you had a mild scrape. This is clearly a cut. How did this happen?"

Sarah diverted her eyes. "I cut it on a broken bottle of medicine. It fell off the dresser when you were . . ."

"When I was what?" he inquired when she paused abruptly.

"Sick. It was just an accident, my own fault really."

"You're lying," John observed while he gingerly cleansed the cut with alcohol. "If you were telling the truth, you would look at me."

"I am *not* a liar," Sarah shot back, facing him. "It was an accident, and if my hands hadn't been wet and slippery, maybe I would've been able to catch the bottle when you knocked it away."

"Knocked it away?" He took a deep breath and forced himself to ask, "Did I hurt you?"

"No, you were just delirious, that's all, severely delirious. I've never seen someone so upset during a fever in all my life. You always seemed to be in so much pain, not only on the outside, but inside as well. You were awake and in a panic, begging me not to leave you and let them take it. I never really understood what you meant. Sometimes, I didn't even think you were the one lying in the bed anymore. You sounded like a little boy."

John found himself shaking as he wrapped a new bandage around Sarah's hand, shocked by her explanation. For years, he had abandoned the little boy he had been, the child who had been so mistreated and neglected. And now, without his control, part of his past had been revealed.

"And you never planned to ask me about it? Dig for details?"

"I was curious," Sarah admitted. "But it was none of my business. And I didn't know if any of it were true or not."

"Then you're the first not to pry," John murmured. "Since I began my career every colleague has looked at me with suspicion and curiosity, wondering how on earth I came to be a doctor without being the son of an aristocrat."

"You won't have to worry about that here. I'm not your colleague and you won't find any aristocrats roaming around."

"What about thieves?" John asked, suddenly growing angry as he remembered the horrible morning he had awakened in the asylum to find that his last family heirloom had been taken, the one he must have been fighting to protect during his delirium.

"Well, no, of course not," Sarah answered.

John smiled as he listened to her, touched by how the idea of stealing had surprised her. "I was a fool to have belittled your tiny town in comparison to Boston. In reality, the kind people here in Templeton could teach people in the city a thing or two. I can't imagine anyone here ever forcing a child to give up their last possession."

"What were you forced to part with, John?" she asked and stroked the side of his face with her fingertips.

Encouraged once again by her sincerity, John muttered, "A watch. A beautiful gold pocket watch my father had ever since he was a child growing up in Europe. It was the only thing he refused to pawn off when we were settling in the East.

"When my parents died of influenza, I was left on my own. All of my parents' relatives were still overseas and didn't have a desire to come be a part of this nation. That's why I know about the asylums I told you about. I was in one briefly."

John heard Sarah give a little cry and felt her hand tremble against his cheek. "I had to relinquish many of my belongings after their deaths. But the pocket watch was one of the few things I could keep and carry around without being weighed down. I thought it would help keep him alive and help me remember."

"Did someone force you to pawn it for money?" Sarah inquired. "So that you could use the money for food?"

John shook his head sadly. "No, it was stolen, flat out stolen."

"Who would steal from an orphaned little boy?"

"A starving grown man," he answered simply. "It happened in one of those asylums I told you about. Though some orphanages are quite horrible, nothing compares to an asylum. There's such a frightening mix of people there. Crazy people by birth, women and men who've turned crazy from starvation and loss of hope, and terrified children from the streets. When you're trapped within those dirty walls, you change. The man who robbed me didn't see me. He only saw my father's watch."

"John, that's horrible. I'm so sorry. No one should have to suffer through something so horrific, especially a child."

"You needn't apologize," he retorted hurriedly. "It was quite some time ago and doesn't effect my life now. I don't expect you to pity me, Sarah."

It was true. He didn't want her pity. How could he allow her to pity him after he had come into town, demanding she turn the only home she had ever known over to him? And why would she pity him? He sighed, abruptly feeling as if he were as horrible a man as the person who stole his father's watch so many years ago.

"I don't pity you," Sarah clarified. "I'm just sorry he took away something that meant so much to you when you were a little boy. I saw you thrashing about during your illness, John. I know it hurt you, and for that, I'm sorry. Pity and sympathy aren't the same thing. Not that I blame you for not wanting my pity. Lately I feel myself growing uneasy from everybody in town giving me pitiful looks. I'm quickly becoming a local charity case."

"I hardly see you as a charity case, Sarah. You're far too independent."

"Thank you, but I'm afraid without a home to call my own, I will be dependent on someone for lodging. But, like you, I do not want pity. Everyone knows that the house was built for the town doctor, and that's your job now."

"Well, I appreciate your compliance, Sarah, but I have been thinking perhaps we should make other arrangements for a while."

"What are you talking about?" Sarah asked as she eased herself off the examining table. "I'm truly sorry my things haven't been packed. Forgive Pap. He thought he was helping me by putting things off. If you could give me a few days to gather a few necessary items together, I could leave the house and stay here."

John nearly winced as he listened to Sarah, reminded of the way he had treated her when they first met and the rude things he had said. "I think it might be best if I stay at the clinic instead for the time being," he told her. "Although I am feeling much better, I don't think I would be up to a ride here every day from Pap Dickens in that thing he calls a wagon."

"That's kind of you, but if it's really just Pap's wagon that has you fearful, you don't need to worry. Like the home, you'll be inheriting my father's wagon and my horse, Thunder."

"Thunder? That doesn't sound like a friendly name."

"Oh, he's very friendly," Sarah insisted. "To me, at least," she added beneath her breath.

"Well, regardless of the friendly horse, I am embarrassed to say I do not know how to drive a wagon."

"Seriously?" Sarah questioned, unable to stifle a chuckle. "I thought all men knew how to drive a wagon, even in cities like Boston. How on earth did you get about?"

"Well, I suppose some men do use wagons, but I was able to walk a great majority of the time. You see, the boardinghouse I stayed in was very close to Saint Francis Hospital. And whenever I went to visit patients at home with Dr. Thompson, he always drove his wagon. I suppose he was so focused on preparing me to be a doctor, he forgot a few simplicities along the way."

"Oh, I see," Sarah replied, "I—" she paused and released a full-out laugh. "Oh, John, I'm sorry! It's just that I've never met a man who couldn't drive a wagon!"

John grinned as he listened to her, hearing her carefree, pure laughter for the first time. He liked the sound of her giggling and seeing her blue eyes free of fear and worry. He chuckled along with her weakly and hoped he would be hearing her laughter many times more.

"So, would you be willing to teach a city boy to drive a wagon?"

"Yes, I think I'm up to the challenge, even though driving you to people in need and not being able to assist in caring for them will be difficult."

"Why wouldn't you assist me? Do you not want to help me?" John asked nervously, surprised by how upset he was by the thought of spending less time with her.

"No, I want to assist you, but you made it pretty clear you want to only work with people who've had proper medical training."

John hung his head. "Oh, I did say that, didn't I? Well, if we're going to be quoting each other, didn't you march up to me and inform me that you would still be assisting me, whether I liked it or not? I may not remember much after that fever set in, but your determination was far too strong to forget."

Sarah nodded. "Yes, I was quite adamant, nearly foolish in my persistence."

"Well, I was quite foolish to treat you so harshly without learning how skilled you were first. Your father was obviously an excellent teacher. So I suggest we call it even. I'll forget your overreactions, if you're willing to forget mine." He offered her his hand. "Do we have a deal?"

"The deal sounds lovely, but I'm not sure I can accept it. While you were ill, I couldn't help but wonder if you had been right about wanting to work with someone who had been to school to study medicine."

"Why would you think that?"

"I panicked before I gave you any medicine. You've thanked me for saving your life, but you should probably be thanking Mrs. North and Pap. Without them, I don't know if I would have ever gotten my bearings and been able to treat you. I couldn't figure out something as simple as a dosage of belladonna on my own without a book or doctor to depend on."

"Regardless of any fear, you still figured it out in time," John reminded her.

"That doesn't matter. I'm just worried it might happen again. I couldn't bear to live with that guilt."

"I think you're being too hard on yourself. You accomplished a lot. You saved my life and had enough sense to request more belladonna from Boston, just in case anyone else would have gotten ill, and now we have it ready to treat other illnesses that cause symptoms similar to scarlet fever. And you kept me isolated to lessen the chance of another outbreak. You would only be doing harm to your town if you stopped assisting."

"Funny how we keep trading places," Sarah whispered. "You came into town determined to live in my house and work with a nurse, and I was determined to keep practicing and refuse to let you live there."

"Things change, people change. So, I think we should forget everything that's happened and start over."

"Very well," Sarah agreed, slipping her uninjured hand into his. "But I insist that you ride out to the house when you're feeling up to it. It would be easier on both of us if we remember this is only temporary. I know that having a home of your own is very important to you."

John nearly shivered when Sarah looked up into his eyes, appearing as if she could see right through him. He wished he could find the courage to give up his dream of finally having a home of his own. Even a bedroom above that clinic would seem like a palace after living in asylums and orphanages and on the streets.

But no matter how he tried, he wasn't ready to part with the home, even for Sarah. It was the one thing in his life that had yet to change—the pain from his childhood ran too deeply to let it.

"Yes," he said, squeezing Sarah's hand before he released it, cherishing her warmth. "I would love to see the house."

Chapter Seven

Sarah drew in a deep breath as Pap's old wagon and faithful donkey traveled over the bumpy hills that led to her childhood home. She took in the scent of wildflowers and pine and watched the dried autumn leaves whirling in the blustery wind.

"You happy to be goin' back to your home, hon?" Pap asked. He paused a moment to look back over his shoulder and snort at John, who sat across from Sarah in the back of the wagon, desperately clinging to the side. "Or, I should say, what was your home before *someone* took it."

Sarah sighed. "I'm not really sure how I feel, Pap. Although, I am very happy to see Thunder again."

"Not as happy as Ned is to not have to see Thunder anymore," Pap muttered. "If I were gone so long from my home in the hills, I woulda gone mad."

"Weeks ago, I was very homesick," she shared, "and wanted to go back to the house so badly to try to find a sense of normalcy again and a break from the epidemic. But now things have changed."

"How so?" John whispered, speaking for the first time during the bumpy ride.

"I guess I realized I couldn't possibly find normalcy there without my father."

"But it's still your home, Sarah," Pap insisted, snorting once more at John. "That's where all your memories are."

"They're not just there, Pap," Sarah replied. "They're inside my mind and my heart. Besides, I'm not certain that house could ever really be a home without Papa there anyway. But maybe John will be able to create some happy memories of his own there."

"That's very kind of you, Sarah," John told her. "If things were reversed, I don't know that I could handle all of this so generously and graciously."

"It wasn't easy," Sarah admitted and then leaned in closer to him to whisper in his ear so Pap wouldn't overhear. "But after hearing about what happened with your father's pocket watch in that terrible asylum, it grew easier. I had a happy childhood and a good home to spend it in. It's time to let someone else find happiness in the house. In time, I'll adjust to the bedroom in the clinic and move on."

"Sarah, you are—whoa!"

John fell forward when the rickety wagon traveled quickly down a steep hill, and he knocked Sarah onto her back. She screamed when she felt her arm dangle over the edge of the open bed and felt herself slipping closer to the ground. But then she saw John's brown eyes gazing down at her, creased in concentration as he wrapped his arm firmly around her waist and lifted her over his own body to shield her from the opening.

She clung to his neck and buried her face in his shoulder, only willing to look up when she felt the wagon come to a complete stop and heard Pap shouting her name.

"Sarah! Sarah, you all right, darlin'?" the old man called out worriedly.

"Y-yes," she stammered and took a deep breath. "I'm fine."

"Are you certain?" John challenged as he ran one hand over her arm. "Did you feel any jerks or pops when your arm dangled? Did you hit your head?"

"No, my arm is fine," she said, bending it to demonstrate. "And so is my head. I'm all right. Just a bit startled."

John tossed a glare up at Pap. "Well, if we had been in a proper wagon this wouldn't have happened!"

"Don't you blame me, city feller!" Pap argued, spitting out the piece of hay in his mouth. "I'm not the one that crushed her like a boulder!"

"Enough!" Sarah shouted over the arguing men. "Honestly, I'm all right, so let's just get back on the trail."

"Well, you heard her, she's all right. That means you can let go of her now, Doc."

Sarah blushed when she realized John was still pressed closely against her with a protective arm around her waist. "Pap's right," she mumbled and instantly sat up and put a few inches between them. "I'll be certain to keep a better grip on the siding, even though it's very doubtful I'll fall off my seat again."

"I lack your faith," John replied, awkwardly pulling himself to the other side of the wagon when they began moving again. "I will never understand how you and Mrs. North tolerate rides with Pap and Lucy so pleasantly."

"The donkey's name is Lulu!" Pap corrected. "It ain't right to forget a lady's name, even a donkey's."

"Please give Lulu my apologies," John muttered.

After a few moments of silence passed, Sarah cleared her throat and whispered. "Thank you for grabbing me back there."

"It wasn't a big deal."

"It was to me. You could have been hurt."

"Being injured myself would have been easier than seeing

you get hurt due to my clumsy mishap. Besides," he added curtly, "it's my job to help others."

Sarah glanced down at her waist, where John's handprint was still indented on her dress from holding her so tightly, and couldn't help but feel his actions had gone beyond the call of duty.

"So, how much longer do you think it will be before we reach the house?"

"Not long at all," she answered and pointed off into the distance at the little house that finally appeared. "That's it. I do hope you'll be satisfied."

"Don't worry, Sarah. After riding in Pap's wagon, anything sitting on land that doesn't move will look heavenly."

Perhaps he said that now, but Sarah couldn't help but wonder if that's truly how John would feel once he saw the home she had shared with her father. She had always found it to be a wonderful place, but had only the other homes in Templeton to compare it to.

She knew from her father's paintings and books how extravagant some of the houses in Boston were. And after being without a home of his own for so long, she imagined John had hoped that the home he would inherit in Templeton would be as ravishing as the ones doctors resided in back East. Nervously, she wrung her hands together while Pap pulled onto the property, and hoped she could control her temper if John was displeased.

Before looking back to see John's expression, she allowed herself to stare at the house. Her eyes gazed over the long boards of dark brown wood, the windows, and the decorative flowers growing all around. She smiled as dozens of happy memories came flooding back.

But when John climbed out of the wagon wordlessly, the memories soon ended. Sarah stared at him, but was unable to read his blank face when he turned to her and stretched his arms out.

"Oh, I'll help Sarah down," Pap butted in, waving away John's hands. "You just go look at the property. Don't want ya to waste any time since it's so important to ya."

"Pap, I told you to stop that!" Sarah whispered, not only annoyed that he had been rude, but that he had ruined her chance to be in John's arms again.

"Ah, I know. But it's awful hard to just sit back and not say a word."

"Don't be upset," Sarah told him as he helped her down. "I'm not. I'll figure something out, Pap, I know I will. But for now, all I want is to stop worrying about the house and visit my horse!"

"You mean Satan's pony," Pap mumbled beneath his breath.

"Thunder! Come on out here, Thunder!" Sarah hollered, running over to the fence as the large black horse emerged from his stable and galloped toward her. "There you are! How I've missed you, my sweet boy!"

"Sweet?" Pap nearly spat. "Sarah, that horse is as sweet as I am young!" Thunder lifted his head and grunted in Pap's direction, then nuzzled gently against Sarah's shoulder.

"That's not true," Sarah defended, stroking Thunder's mane. "He's just particular, that's all. My, how handsome you look. Ned has done a wonderful job keeping you well fed, hasn't he?"

"Amazin' Thunder didn't eat Ned," Pap chimed in. "I can't wait to see how he feels about our new city feller."

"I'm sure Thunder will be polite if John is," Sarah said with false confidence. "And even though I could probably spend the rest of the day here spoiling him, I better go catch up with John. I'm sure he'd like to see more of the house than just the outside," she added, looking over her shoulder at John while he observed the home's exterior and the land surrounding it.

"You'd think he'd already seen it, the way he claimed it so

quick," Pap grumbled. "But don't you let that wear you down, darlin'. I'm gonna need me a partner for some good old-fashioned jigs tonight at the barn dance. You were plannin' on headin' out to the Gibsons', weren't ya?"

"Naturally. May would never forgive me if I missed it."

"Well, I'll be by later to give ya a ride on up there. Unless somebody else already offered."

"Reverend Harrin mentioned something about it, but I haven't heard from him today with any further details, so I'd love to ride with you and Mrs. North. But would you mind coming by the clinic? Maybe we could all go there and persuade John to go with us."

"Why would we wanna do that?"

"Because it's the right thing to do. John's going to continue to be an outsider in Templeton until we all get a chance to know him and he gets a chance to know us. Besides, after being sick for so long, he needs an opportunity to have a little fun."

"Oh, all right then," Pap relented, climbing up into his wagon. "I guess the city feller can tag along if he wants. I do like watchin' him get all riled up about my drivin'."

"Oh, Pap, you don't fool me for one minute, you tender-hearted old man," she said and blew him a kiss. "I'll see you tonight."

As Pap drove away, Sarah started up the hill and called out to John, "The door should be open. You can go in, you don't need to wait for me!"

John shook his head. "No, I'll wait. I think I should meet this horse of yours first. I haven't spent much time with horses since I was a very young boy, and I might as well start getting used to it again now. After all, they are essential to driving a wagon."

"Oh, but that can wait!" Sarah insisted. "Thunder isn't going anywhere."

"Neither is the house. I thought you said he was friendly?"

Sarah smiled, comforted by all the things the thankful townspeople had given to her family over the years to make their home a beautiful one. Even now, despite the thin layers of dust that had collected while she had been staying in town, the house looked as lovely as it always had, at least in her eyes.

She turned her head and was greeted by a blank expression on John's face. She shivered slightly, worried by his silence. Despite all the wonderful decorations, he hadn't said one nice thing about the home. She desperately wanted him to say something, even if it meant griping about Thunder and acting the way he did when he'd first arrived in town.

Swiftly, Sarah cleared her throat, determined to make John realize what a fine home he was inheriting, regardless of the mansions he had seen in Boston. "I know it may not seem like much to you," she announced loudly, "but it really is quite a nice home. Many people around here think it's practically a palace. Windows and a wooden floor may seem common to you, but they're actually a luxury here. And there's a comfortable loft, Papa's bed is practically brand new, and—"

"Sarah," John intervened, "you don't have to try to make this home sound lovely. I know it is. I love it."

"Y-you do?" Sarah stammered. "You were being so quiet, I was afraid you were disappointed."

"No, I was not disappointed," John murmured, "I was speechless. It's a lovely home, clean and comfortable. It will be the nicest place I have ever lived in."

Sarah felt her heart fill with warmth and a nagging bit of regret. "I'm glad you like it."

"And correct me if I'm wrong, but am I smelling peppermint? It's the oddest thing, I could have sworn I was smelling it at the clinic too."

"You were. It's a favorite of mine that my father kept around."

"Well, then I'll have to remember to keep it in stock," John replied with a smile as he walked around. "The craftsmanship of this furniture is simply remarkable," he complimented. "Did your father have this sent in from Boston?"

"No, actually, a local carpenter made it several years ago as payment for the delivery after his wife gave birth."

"Payment? Why didn't he just pay with money?"

"He couldn't afford it. Few people can. But don't worry, everyone's always paid their debts somehow. You'll never go hungry or have to worry about a place to stay or even when to buy new curtains. Do you think you could adapt to that lifestyle, Dr. Carson?"

"I told you to call me John and, yes, I could. I'm not quite the tyrant you think I am, Sarah. Back in Boston I tried to treat many of the downtrodden citizens, and I never got a penny or curtain in return."

No, Sarah thought, he certainly wasn't a tyrant anymore. Or, at least, this new John Carson wasn't. Ever since he had woken up from his delirium, he had acted like a different person, a better person—but even then it was as if there were a brick wall built around him to keep her away every time she seemed to get too close.

Tiredly, Sarah shook her head. She simply had to stop thinking about him so deeply. It was a waste of time and completely foolish.

"The paintings that are hanging up are from Boston," she said suddenly, pointing to the pictures on the wall. "But I'm sure you already presumed that from the landmarks."

"Ah, they're wonderful. Your father must have had them brought in to remember his first home."

"Not exactly. He bought them because my mother adored them. She was a simple country girl who had never seen or heard of a place with so many people and things to do, and she was always curious about Boston. Papa came from a wealthy family, so he had the paintings made as an elaborate Christmas present. That was before he lost contact with his brother."

"He must have loved your mother deeply to go to all that trouble."

"Yes, he did," Sarah said. "But there's no sense in talking about Papa and his things. They're yours now."

"Not everything," John protested, looking up at her. "Everything in here is yours. They're your family heirlooms."

Sarah stared back at him for a moment, touched by the reverence that filled his voice and shone in his brown eyes. "Well, thank you," she said, forcing herself to look away from him. "But I simply won't be able to keep everything. And I insist you take the paintings. They're lovely, but they won't do me much good. There's really only a few things I truly want. A few of Papa's belongings, my clothes, naturally. But I promise to begin getting things in order for you so that you'll have more space and can begin moving your things in. I'll look through the old trunks up in the loft soon to see if there's any of my mother's dresses May would want or that other women could use in the wedding. That should undo a lot of clutter."

"Your mother's dresses? You mean, you would just give them to May?" John asked, his voice raised slightly.

"Well, of course. She's my dearest friend. And she would love to have a fancy wedding dress. It will make her happy."

"But what about you?" John prodded. "You should be the one wearing those dresses. There's a part of your mother in them."

"Yes, I suppose there is, but I've never really had any reason to wear such fancy dresses."

"Not even to a dance? I could have sworn I heard people talking about a dance in town when we left the clinic. Was I mistaken?"

"There is a dance, the dance out at the Gibson farm that I told you about. Are you planning to attend? You were invited, you know. I'm sure everyone would love to see you and see that you're doing so much better, and thank you properly for everything you've done. Or are you still afraid that we dance on pig droppings?"

"No." John laughed heartily. "I know you would never dance on pig droppings. But are you sure people want me there? It's quite obvious that Pap isn't too fond of me."

"Oh, don't let Pap get to you. Plenty of people want you there. Even Ned, and his family is hosting the dance."

"What about you?"

"What about me?" Sarah asked uneasily, both flattered and nervous when John locked eyes with her.

"Do you want me there?"

"Um . . . well . . . I . . . Of course I want you there. It would be good for you, like I said."

"All right then," John answered. "I'll be there. But if I get dizzy trying to square dance, I'm holding you responsible."

"It's a risk I'm willing to take," Sarah replied and backed away from him before she lost her composure. "Come on, I'll show you the loft."

Carefully, she climbed the ladder, smiling when she felt John's hands grip around her waist for added support.

"Did you use this as a bedroom?" he asked.

"Yes," Sarah answered with a smile, comforted to be in her own room again. "I know it's small, but it was my sanctuary over the years. I loved Papa dearly, but everyone needs their own space."

"Indeed they do," John agreed grimly. "Though I'm amazed you had any room for a bed amongst all the stuff up here."

Sarah tenderly ran her hand over one of the many old trunks. "Papa never could part with my mother's things, no matter how much space they consumed. As silly as it sounds, he could never bear to open them, either. Maybe that's part of the reason I never wore her dresses—to keep from hurting him. He always told me I looked a lot like my mother. Seeing me in her clothing may have been too much for him."

"And what about you? Do you think it might be too much for you?"

"I don't really know," Sarah admitted and sat down on her bed. "I never grew overly emotional when I took the dresses out to look at them and try my best to clean them." She lifted a brow and faced him. "Why are you being so persistent? I really don't understand why you care so much about dresses."

"It's not the dresses," John assured her as he sat down on one of the trunks. "It's the feeling that comes with it. You remember the pocket watch I told you about, my father's?"

She nodded.

"I would have given anything to have had that watch to hold and look at on rough days during my childhood, and even now. I'm sure it sounds materialistic and even selfish, but it made me feel like a little part of my family hadn't been taken away from me, even after my father's death. As long as I could see that watch, I would remember my father's face when he looked at it. And now I can't really remember it. That's why I've been so persistent about your mother's dresses," he explained.

"Sarah, I know the pain that comes with the loss of your parents, and even though I've seen how strong you are, I know tonight may be hard for you. I just thought wearing one of your mother's dresses that your father had seen her in might help make it a bit easier. Forgive me if I was overzealous."

"No, not at all," Sarah replied, nearly awestruck by his heartfelt candor. "Maybe I will consider it, and even open the trunks right now. I haven't taken out her dresses in ages. I barely remember what they look like."

John stood. "You should look at them on your own. I might have gotten sentimental thinking about a pocket watch, but I'm still masculine enough that gawking at frilly gowns doesn't appeal to me. I'll go downstairs and look around for a while, maybe try to find where you hide your peppermints."

"All right," Sarah said with a chuckle.

"And Sarah?" John added as he started down the ladder.

"Yes?"

"Maybe you should wear your hair down instead of in a braid tonight, if you wear one of those fancy gowns."

"And when did the town doctor start caring about how women wear their hair? I'll have you know I wasn't planning on wearing a braid. I was going to wear my hair up like most women do."

"You forgot one thing, Sarah. You aren't like most women."

"That was one of the most frightening experiences of my life!" John Carson exclaimed when he burst into the Gibsons' barn, gasping for air.

"Dr. Carson, are you all right?" May worried, dragging Ned along with her as she rushed to his side. "What happened?"

"I have had a life-changing experience, more frightening than any epidemic or bout with scarlet fever could ever be!"

"What he means," Pap Dickens said calmly as he sauntered into the barn and escorted Mrs. North inside, "is that he rode over here in my wagon."

"Wagon," John scoffed. "More like the carriage of death, I'd say! And riding in it is a thousand times worse at night. At least in daylight you can see and attempt to prepare yourself for the near-collisions. Excuse me, May, could you please tell me if there is any water nearby? I would like some to refresh myself."

May pointed to a table in the corner. "There's some cider over there."

"Thank you," John replied gratefully.

"What a city boy," Ned grunted, rolling his eyes as he pulled May closer to him. "Can't even ride in a wagon without gettin' all riled up."

"And he don't know how to treat ladies proper," Pap

chimed in. "Why, I was right excited when Sarah accepted the Reverend Harrin's offer to bring her here."

"Reverend Harrin?" May gasped, swallowing roughly. "*He's* bringing Sarah?"

"Yes, he rode over to Sarah's house and asked her," Mrs. North explained uneasily. "It was kind of him to let Pap know beforehand so he wouldn't drive all the way over."

"That's because the Reverend knows how to treat ladies. Folks shouldn't be fillin' Sarah's head with ideas about that city feller when there's a man like Reverend Harrin around."

"Well, I hate to be rude to y'all, but Ned and I have a few more decorations we need to put up before everybody gets here," May announced.

"We do?" Ned asked, dumbfounded.

"Yes!" May whispered into his ear and tugged roughly on his arm to pull him away.

"Gosh, May, what are ya gettin' all angry about?"

She planted her hands on her hips. "This ruins our whole plan! Why aren't you more upset? We had it all worked out for John and Sarah to arrive together and spend time with one another tonight! Don't you remember askin' her to stick around him?"

"Ah, I can't remember any of that. You know I just did it because you asked me to. I don't care. Though Pap's got a darn good point—at least the Reverend wouldn't kick Sarah out of her home, for Pete's sake. He's a good man."

"Of course he's a good man, but he's also nearly sixty. Sarah shouldn't be courted by someone older than her pa was. Now, I know every year all the guys in town are real nice about askin' Sarah to dance so she don't feel so lonesome. Did you remember to tell 'em all to leave her alone this time?"

"Well, the only thing I've really had on my mind about the whole barn dance was getting to spend time with you now that you're all better and wonderin' what kinds of pies women would be bringin'."

"Ned, how could you think about food?" May groaned. "Now all the men are gonna ask Sarah to dance and all the young, unhitched girls in town are gonna have their mas settin' them up to dance with John!"

"Maybe it's fer the best. If people don't get together on their own, maybe they just ain't meant to be together."

"You hold your tongue, Ned Gibson!" May ordered, crossing her arms. "Did you forget your ma is the one that got us courtin'?"

"Oh," Ned mumbled sheepishly, feeling his cheeks burn. "In that case, I'll just go tell some of the fellers that are already here to ease off Sarah this year."

"You're too late!" May sighed when Reverend Harrin stepped into the barn, escorting Sarah on his arm. "You just go eat your pie!" she ordered and hurried over to Sarah.

"Sarah, don't you look pretty!"

"Do I, May?" Sarah asked, looking down nervously.

"Of course you do! You know, someone was looking for you. Reverend Harrin, please forgive me, but you do mind if I steal Sarah for a while?"

"Oh, of course not," the Reverend replied, releasing Sarah's arm. "Visit for as long as you like."

"Who's looking for me?" Sarah inquired as May dragged her through the barn.

"John. He just don't know it yet."

"What?"

"Look, John! Sarah's here and I know you were wantin' to see her."

"May, I didn't—" John gasped and quickly shut his mouth when he turned around and saw Sarah.

In all of his life, he had never seen someone look so lovely. Though the other women in town had put on their finest dresses, none of them could compare to Sarah. Slowly, he gazed at the pale pink gown that hung to the floor, decorated with ruffles, bows, and slightly puffed sleeves. A string of pearls were bound around her neck, and her blond hair lay in loose curls, dangling over her shoulders.

"You didn't what?" Sarah questioned quietly.

"I didn't mean for May to drag you over here, that's all," John answered, "but I'm glad she did."

"I knew you would be," May stated brightly and gave Sarah a gentle nudge toward him. "You two chitchat; I'm gonna go find Ned."

"Cider?" John offered.

"No, thank you. I don't want to risk spilling any on my mother's dress. I bet it looked much more becoming on her," Sarah said. She swallowed roughly while she stared down at the gown. "Do I look as foolish as I feel? Are people staring?"

"Yes," John told her, looking at all of the men and women in the barn turning their way. "People are staring. Everyone is staring."

"I knew this was a bad idea!" Sarah panicked. "They're probably staring at me, angry that I wore something so fancy, knowing very well no one else possibly could. I do hope I haven't hurt anyone's feelings."

"Sarah," John said soothingly, taking her gloved hand, "people aren't staring because they're jealous. They're staring because you are beautiful."

John strained his neck while he danced in circles with May, struggling to see Sarah as Pap whirled her around the dance floor, despite the slow music. All night, they had been kept apart, when men had asked Sarah to dance one after the other and women had pushed their unmarried daughters at him.

Only weeks ago, the idea of women nearly fighting to have their daughters dance in his arms would have been thrilling. But now, the only woman he wanted to dance with was Sarah.

"What kind of steps are those?" May asked suddenly. "I can't follow you."

"Oh, um, it's the waltz," John mumbled back distractedly, looking down at his feet.

She sighed and stood still. "It looks awful fancy. I'm afraid I just can't follow you."

"I apologize. I just did it instinctively. We could try something else."

"Oh, that's all right, we just need to trade partners, that's all," May declared, walking him across the dance floor.

"Excuse me?"

"Oh, don't worry, it's nothin' personal. You just need to dance with Sarah. She knows how to do those fancy dances—her pa taught her. Hey, Pap!" she called out to the energetic old man. "You mind if I cut in?"

"Well, if Sarah don't mind, it's all right with me, darlin'," Pap replied, eyeing John steadily. "You make sure you don't step on Sarah's feet, city feller!"

"I'll do my best," John promised as he traded places with Pap. "Are you all right with the switch, Sarah?"

"I'm very happy with it," Sarah responded, sliding her hand into his. "I mean, it's awfully hard to keep up with Pap all night. Were you waltzing earlier?"

"Yes, you're familiar with it?"

"Vaguely. I haven't done it in a while."

"Neither have I. Maybe between the two of us we can remember it all. Shall we dance?"

"Yes," Sarah replied and effortlessly followed his lead.

Together, they danced around, oblivious to the other couples and nearly floating on air. For a moment, while John stared at Sarah in her fancy dress and waltzed, he almost felt like a dream had come true. The townspeople were watching him as he made each turn, looking at him with respect and admiration. In a small way, he felt like his colleagues in Boston he had both hated and admired.

But when he glanced down at Sarah, studying her warm smile and taking in the sweet smell of her hair, his dream of being wealthy and respected suddenly didn't seem so important. He drew Sarah closer and began to wonder if the time had come to begin making new dreams for his life.

"John . . . John," Sarah said, bringing him back to reality.

"Hmm?" he mumbled.

"The music stopped," she told him quietly.

"Oh, I'm sorry," John apologized and stopped quickly. "I must have been thinking of something else, I suppose."

"Don't be embarrassed. You weren't the only one not to notice," Sarah commented, watching Pap still twirling and stomping around. "Would you like to step outside?" she asked and turned to face him once again. "You're looking a little flushed. Is it getting too warm in here for you?"

John brought his hands to his cheeks, knowing the redness had come from holding Sarah and not from a stuffy barn. "Yes, I'd like that very much."

John trailed behind her, breathing in the night air when they stepped outside. He exhaled slowly and tilted his head up to look at the sky twinkling with stars and glowing with moonlight.

"Isn't it beautiful?" Sarah said. "My papa always said there was nothing on earth that could be as breathtaking as a full moon in the fall. The harvest moon, he called it."

"It is a nice sight," John agreed, looking down at Sarah, "but I believe there are other things on earth I'd rather look at. You're a vision in that gown," he blurted out before he could stop himself.

Sarah turned away shyly. "Thank you. I'm glad I listened to you. Wearing it did help me feel a little closer to my mother, even though I never really knew her. And, naturally, that helps me remember Papa."

"You must be missing him right now, during this annual barn dance."

"A little," Sarah admitted. "But being here with you—," she said, clearing her throat quickly. "I meant, being here waltzing with you has made it easier. It was nice to remember waltzing and imagining what my mother must have felt like, dancing in this dress with him."

"Your father must have been the envy of the town to have her on his arm, just like Reverend Harrin tonight."

"Reverend Harrin? What are you talking about, John?"

"Your escort," John replied bluntly, not even attempting to hide his jealousy.

"Reverend Harrin is hardly my escort. He is merely a kind man who took pity on me just as everyone else did tonight. Do you think I'm a fool? I know very well why I'm asked to dance over and over. It's because everyone feels sorry for Sarah Bethel, the doctor's daughter and future old maid of Templeton. Even though none of the men in town ever wanted to court me, that doesn't mean they aren't willing to take turns dancing with me. It's the same thing every year, even when Papa was alive. He always thought it was because I was the belle of the ball, but I knew the truth."

"That can hardly be true, Sarah," John argued. "You must be aware of how attractive you are. The men were probably too afraid to ask you for more than a dance. Perhaps your father intimidated them."

"You sound like May and couldn't be more wrong. Men aren't interested in women who assist doctors instead of cooking, and Papa was far from intimidating. He was tall, lanky, and shy."

"Well, at least this year you weren't alone." John laughed weakly. "Women must have felt obligated to keep the unmarried city boy doctor on the dance floor too."

"No, it's different for men. You've been the talk of Templeton for weeks, the ideal husband."

"I'm far from the ideal husband," John replied, rolling his eyes. "I don't know that I even want to be a husband."

"Really?" Sarah practically gasped. "You didn't come to Templeton with the hope of starting a family in your new home?"

"Not at all. I just wanted the house and a chance to finally get out of Boston. Right now I want to focus on beginning my practice and adjusting to life out here," he answered, noticing the sad glint that shimmered in Sarah's eyes. "But if it happened, I guess I could try to be open to it," he added, even though he knew it was lie. He would never be able to love any woman enough to marry her and start a family. It was impossible for him to trust anyone enough to ever give them his heart fully. "What about you, Sarah? What do you want?"

"I just want to be happy, I guess," Sarah mumbled, shivering when the wind grew stronger.

John instantly unbuttoned the jacket of his suit and slid it down his arms. "You guess? I wouldn't think the thought of being happy would take much consideration."

"John, you of all people should know happiness is sometimes less important than stability and dealing with real life." Sarah smiled when the jacket touched her shoulders and lifted her hands to wrap it tighter. "Thank you."

John stood quietly for a moment, keeping his hands firmly on the jacket, allowing Sarah's fingers to meet his and their faces to be only inches apart. He wanted to start screaming at himself to move and let go, and quit gazing at her beauty. He had to stop thinking and worrying about her all the time and cast a blind eye to her pretty face. Nothing would ever come from his attraction to her.

But it was too late now. He couldn't turn away from her. Not now, when he was finally so close to her, close enough to feel her pulse racing from her wrist and thumping against his fingertips, her breath grazing his neck. He realized he wanted to touch more than her hands as he glanced at her soft, pink lips.

"Maybe I can tell you something that would make you happy," he muttered into her ear.

"What's that?" she asked breathlessly.

"It's time that men started seeing you differently," he answered, taking her face in his hands and turning her toward him. "It's time they stop seeing you as only the doctor's daughter and a future old maid," he explained and pressed his lips against hers, giving her a kiss that, despite its sweet innocence, was filled with deep passion.

Chapter Eight

O h, Sarah, this dress is just beautiful!" May squealed as she climbed down the loft ladder with a white gown, layered with lace, draped over her shoulder. "I couldn't have even pictured up a prettier dress in my head. Thank you again for lettin' me come over and pick out one."

"Mmm-hmm," Sarah mumbled, staring off absently while she continued sewing a rip in one of her mother's old dresses by the fireplace.

"Sarah!" May exclaimed and pulled the away the clothing in her lap. "Stop sewin'—you pricked yourself."

"Oh," Sarah said, quickly coming to her senses when she looked down at her bloody finger. "I'm sorry, May, I didn't even notice. I may know a few things about stitching injuries, but I am still useless with clothes."

"How could you notice with your head in the clouds? Did you even look at the weddin' gown I picked out?"

"Well, not closely," Sarah confessed sheepishly, taking a more observant look when May removed the gown from her shoulder and held it out. "Oh, May, it is lovely. You'll look very beautiful in that, it really suits you. Ned will be speechless."

May giggled. "Well, that doesn't mean much. You know he never is good with words, anyway. But it will be nice to get to wear somethin' so fancy on our special day."

"Why don't you go slip it on?" Sarah suggested. "I may be a poor seamstress, but with your help, I think I can manage to mark any needed alterations and make things easier for your mother to hem."

"Oh, don't fret about that. I've got more important things to figure out."

"Like what?"

"Like figurin' out why your mind's been somewhere else all day long, Sarah, I only wish I knew where. You look so happy, I'd like to go there too!"

"I'm not happy," Sarah answered immediately, refusing to admit she had been thinking about the kiss she and John had shared at the barn dance the night before. "I was just thinking."

"Thinkin' about somethin' romantic, I bet," May presumed. "Don't tell me you've got feelin's for Reverend Harrin!"

"No, nothing beyond friendship," Sarah answered honestly.

"Then it's John you're dreamin' about! Oh, I knew it. I just knew you two belonged together. And Ned said I shouldn't be matchmakin'."

"I never said I was thinking about John."

"But you never said you weren't," May teased.

"Oh, fine," Sarah relented. "I was thinking about John."

"Ain't a surprise considerin' the way you two were lookin' at each other last night, dancin' around without noticing another person. Why, he didn't even know when the music stopped, he was so busy starin' at you lookin' so beautiful last night."

"Oh, that's nonsense, May. I didn't look beautiful."

"Uh-huh," May grumbled with a roll of her eyes, "and Ned

didn't eat fifteen pieces of pie. Don't you try to fool me, Sarah, it was plain as day you two were fallin' head over heels. Why, when you two came back inside after you disappeared in the moonlight, I figured I wouldn't be the only one plannin' to get hitched."

"A little kiss hardly leads to a marriage proposal."

"Kiss!" May exclaimed, tossing her wedding dress aside. "You kissed him? And you let me babble on about a dress instead of tellin' me? You stop sewin' right now and tell me each little thing."

"What's to tell?" Sarah said nervously, embarrassed she had admitted she'd allowed John to kiss her so soon. "Our lips touched. The end."

"Oh, fiddlesticks the end!"

"Don't go on about it, May, I feel badly enough as it is."

"Bad? You mean, you didn't like kissin' him?"

"No!" Sarah said, exasperated. "I just feel silly, that's all. We haven't even been properly courting and I just let him kiss me. I should've had a little more control."

"Sarah, the two of you spent weeks workin' side by side savin' lives during an outbreak. Heck, you saved *his* life. I think you can overlook courtin'. And you've never done anything that ain't proper in your life."

"I doubt using excuses is proper."

"It's not an excuse, it's the truth. If you feel so bad about it, just start courtin'."

"Oh, it's not that simple, is it?" Sarah questioned. "I mean, doesn't the man have to ask the girl?"

"If I waited around for that, Ned and I wouldn't be gettin' hitched. Now, I know our fellers like to think they're in control, but sometimes a gal's just got to give a little push to get things goin' in the right direction. His ma's the one that set him straight. But since your ma's passed, I'd be happy to talk to John."

"Oh, no! No!" Sarah refused automatically. "Thank you,

but I really don't think that approach would work with John. In fact, it might scare him all the way back to Boston. But you do have a point. I guess there isn't any harm in telling him exactly where I stand and that I am not the kind of girl who will just kiss any man, let alone keep on doing it without knowing his intentions. After all, I did promise I'd help him learn how to handle a wagon today."

"That's the spirit!" May praised, clapping her hands. "I can't wait to tell Mrs. North that you and John are finally seein' what's so clear."

"May, don't you dare. That isn't—"

"I know, it isn't proper. Fine, fine, I'll keep my mouth shut."

"Why are you going to see Mrs. North? She hasn't taken ill, has she?"

"Ah, no, nothin' like that. She just told me at the dance that I should come over and look at some old jewelry she had. Between your ma's beautiful dress and Mrs. North's pretty jewelry, I really am gonna look like a princess, huh?"

Sarah reached out and hugged her. "Indeed, and a beautiful one. Oh, I'm getting so excited for you!"

"Don't waste that on me, you save it for John. In fact, you go see him right now and I'll go visit Mrs. North."

"May, do you think you could take her something for me?" Sarah requested, reaching into her pocket and gripping the letter she had written days ago but never mailed.

"Of course I can."

"Thank you," Sarah said meekly and handed her the envelope with a shaky hand.

"Walter Bethel, New York," May read aloud. "Is that the uncle you told me about?"

Sarah nodded. "Yes. I only hope I'm doing the right thing writing him. Naturally, I had to tell him about Papa's passing. Even if they lost touch, that doesn't stop them from being brothers. But maybe I shouldn't have told him about my situation here and the house going to John. He'll probably think I'm only writing him for money."

"No, he won't. And even if he does, you said he's an architect. He can send you some money and still have plenty."

"*Aristocrat,* May."

"Oh, whatever," May said with a careless shrug. "And maybe it won't even matter what your uncle thinks if you and John get to courtin'. You could just get hitched and live together."

"Don't get ahead of yourself, May," Sarah warned as she put away her sewing supplies. "But I am going to go see him right now," she declared, deciding she would stop worrying what her estranged uncle will think of her and focus on finding out what John Carson thought of her instead.

"Pull on the reins, John!" Sarah hollered when their wagon swerved dangerously over grassy hills and slopes.

"I am!" John shouted back, pulling with all his might. "But this demonic horse of yours won't slow down!"

"Don't call Thunder demonic!" Sarah snapped as she clung to her seat.

"Sarah, now really isn't the time to argue about the horse's temper when he's trying to kill us!"

"Give me the reins!" Sarah ordered and ripped them out of his hands. "Thunder!" she shouted angrily, giving the reins a firm tug. "You stop right now!" she demanded.

As soon as he heard his owner's voice, Thunder ended his lightning-fast run and slowed to a gallop and, finally, to a complete stop.

"How—how did you do that?" John gasped.

"Easily," Sarah replied. "You just have to let Thunder know who is the boss. I told you he takes orders. And to think you called him demonic."

"Are you forgetting he ruined another one of my hats?" John protested. "Knocked it right off my head and started stomping on it!"

Sarah stood and began to climb out of the wagon seat. "Perhaps one day you'll learn to stop wearing them around him."

"Wait, I'll help you," John offered and jumped down.

"I'm sure I can manage."

"As you often tell me, learn to let someone help you," John replied, balancing his hands on her waist as she slid down. He swallowed hard when her hands gripped his shoulders and her skirt brushed against his legs. Suddenly, being so close, it felt like they were reliving last night, and he longed to kiss her once again.

Sarah's eyes locked with his, and as he looked into her gaze, he knew she felt the same. But before he could act on his feelings, she had already broken out of their embrace and went to Thunder's side to stroke his mane.

John cleared his throat awkwardly, partially thankful that Sarah had enough sense to break away before they kissed again. But he hated that she had returned to her uncharacteristic silence. Shockingly, he had actually been grateful to Thunder for his recklessness. It was the only thing that had sparked a word from Sarah since she had offered to take him on his first driving lesson.

"You were brave to bring me out in these hills," he commented randomly. "I guess we should have stayed in town and tried safer trails."

"Maybe," Sarah retorted. "But you'll rarely need to drive in town. It's hills like these you'll have to deal with when you make house calls. And in just a little while, Gertie Patten will be having her baby, and the hills out by her cabin are much worse than the ones you practiced on today."

"Yes, she should be having the baby any day now. I just hope we won't end up on her doorstep needing medical treatment ourselves due to my lack of skill as a driver."

John cursed beneath his breath when Sarah only gave him a weak smile in return. He had desperately wanted to make her laugh and see a glimpse of the girl who intrigued him. "Are you all right?" he asked slowly.

"Of course I am."

"You just . . . seem like you have something on your mind," John managed to choke out.

"I imagine it's the same thing that's on your mind," Sarah said, looking up at him. "I guess if we want to stop being so awkward around one another, we're going to have to talk about last night. I'm sorry if I seemed cold. I was just hoping you would bring it up first."

"What's to talk about? We just kissed. I mean, it's not that uncommon for a man and woman to kiss after a dance."

"Maybe it's not uncommon for you, but it certainly is uncommon for me. I am not in the habit of randomly kissing men. I don't know what type of woman you think I am, but I can assure you I am not the type to go around sharing something as special as a kiss with just anyone. And now I'm even more embarrassed to know that I let myself be foolish enough to not only kiss someone I barely know, but to know you don't even think kissing is special!"

Special? John hardly thought their kiss had been special. He thought their kiss had been magical and frightening. The moment he had kissed Sarah, he felt everything he had sworn he would never allow himself to feel.

"I do think kissing is special, Sarah," John whispered, unable to look at her when he said the words. "But I am sorry for whatever discomfort it caused you. Just so you know, I would never think you are the type of girl who would behave radically and without sense. I am the one at fault for what happened. Now, hopefully, we can forget about it and move on."

"I'm not sure I can forget, John," Sarah admitted softly. "Believe me, I wish I could. It would make things so much easier. But forgetting isn't something I can do easily."

"Then you certainly are a rarity. Most people easily forget about me," John replied, unable to hide the resentment from his voice as he briefly recalled his horrific past in Boston.

Sarah stepped closer and looked directly into his eyes. "Maybe that's why I can't just forget about you. There were times when I tried, because I was tired of feeling like a silly schoolgirl, but I never succeeded. It's impossible to forget someone when inside all you really want is to know more about them."

John blinked but held her gaze, too mesmerized by her sapphire eyes to turn away. So, she had been trying to forget just as passionately as he had and had also failed miserably.

What was it about this woman that always enabled her to see through him? He was surprised she had any questions to ask him, considering he often wondered if she was capable of reading his mind.

"I should've assumed you would want to know more. I mean, after all, I gave you vivid details about asylums and a stolen pocket watch. How could you not have questions? I do give you credit for approaching me. People back in Boston just provided dirty looks. And—"

"Would you stop talking for one blasted minute?!" Sarah snapped, planting her hands on her hips. "I'm not like the people back in Boston who shunned you because you weren't an aristocrat, and you know it, so don't treat me like one of them. I don't want to know more about you because I'm curious, I want to know more about you because I care."

John locked his knees, suddenly feeling light on his feet when Sarah finished speaking. It had been so long since he had known someone deeply cared for him, he couldn't remember the natural way to respond.

"I'm sorry," Sarah said after a few silent moments had passed. "I only wanted to know more about the man with whom I shared my first kiss. I guess it was silly and even childish. I certainly didn't mean for things to get so intense. Please accept my apology."

John released a ragged breath as he watched Sarah walk away and kneel down in front of the creek to dab cool water on her flushed face. While he gazed at her, he thought of the night during the epidemic when he revealed a bit of his past to her. Talking with her and sharing some of the memories he had been so desperate to forget had calmed him. And despite his instinctive hesitancy, he knew if he opened up to her again, he would undoubtedly feel relieved and refreshed.

John walked to her side and sat down. "I would be happy to accept your apology, if you had anything to apologize for. But you don't. Go ahead and ask me your questions. I shouldn't have gotten angry, I'm flattered you find me so intriguing."

"Don't put words in my mouth," Sarah told him, unable to hide a smile. "I never said you were intriguing, I just said I cared."

"All right, so what do you care to find out about?" John asked.

"Just a few more details to fill out the bits and pieces that I already know," Sarah clarified. "I know that you were trained by a doctor and that you spent a little time in an asylum after your parents died. But that leaves a lot still hidden. How did you manage to become a doctor when you didn't have a penny to your name? How did you leave the asylum?"

"It's not exactly an entertaining fairy tale."

"I wasn't expecting it to be. The truth rarely is."

John shut his eyes and drew in a deep breath. "I was in the asylum for weeks with the rest of the homeless who had been taken off the streets, practically starving to death. But then a couple came, Mr. and Mrs. Wilder, and told the people in charge that they wanted to start an orphanage for boys on their property."

"You mentioned them when you were delirious with fever. You seemed very fearful of them."

He sighed bitterly. "I wish I had been when I first met them. I can still remember the loads of freshly baked bread they brought us, and boys were fighting to get them, to be one of the lucky ones to leave. Only we weren't lucky at all.

"There were six of us huddled in the back of their wagon, nearly falling out, thinking we were going to be living like kings. We got to their land and saw this big, old house and we all went running to it excitedly—then the yelling started, the incessant yelling. They moved all of us into the attic and started handing out chores. They didn't want to help children. They just wanted servants."

John paused a moment to collect himself as the sordid memories flashed before him. "We milked cows, cleaned floors, tended to their land, cooked their food. So many of us barely knew what we were doing, and accidents happened. Cuts, burns. That's how I got to meet Dr. Thompson.

"I had gone into town with another boy to buy some food and Dr. Thompson saw us in the store and questioned how we got some of our injuries. I can't remember what nonsense we rattled off, but he was very calm and followed us home. He came into the Wilders' home, making it known that he wouldn't be leaving until we received medical treatment. He was suave about it all, almost making it look as if they were the victims, unable to get all of us to a doctor. Even as a child, I knew he loathed them, and was impressed by his ability to disguise it so well.

"He mesmerized me, treating our cuts and scrapes, checking for infections. It had been so long since I had seen anyone in the world do something good. I felt like I was watching a miracle and I knew I wanted to be like him.

"He came to check on us every week. And, as time passed, he noticed how intensely I watched him. When I was a little older and becoming a young man, he taught me some simple procedures I could do to help the other boys if they got hurt while he was away."

"That's amazing," Sarah said. "You were a child yourself and taking care of children."

John shrugged. "It was what needed to be done and what I wanted to do. Dr. Thompson was impressed by my dedication, telling me many times that I needed to be in school so I could become a real doctor."

"You weren't allow to attend school, John?"

"No, if we attended school, we weren't there to tend to the Wilders. But Dr. Thompson had a plan of his own to offer those lowlifes. One day he informed them it was time to pay their debts for all the services he had provided. Of course, they went ballistic—and he easily calmed them when he said he would waive his fees if they allowed me to leave with him. Naturally, they agreed."

"They traded you like you were a bag of sugar?" Sarah exclaimed.

John smiled, touched as he always was when she was shocked and disgusted by the realities of the world he had known. "Yes, but it was the best thing they ever did for me. Dr. Thompson didn't see me as a bag of sugar. He just knew suggesting a trade would provide a way to get me out of there so I could live with him. He offered to take me in as long as I promised to earn my keep."

"You were turned into a servant again?" Sarah asked as a tear trickled down her cheek.

John reached out to wipe away her tear. "No. He only expected me to attend school and accompany him on some of his patient visits to learn more, so that he could help me get into medical school."

"Like a father figure?"

"Sort of. It wasn't the same bond that I had shared with my father. I knew I was the doctor's student and apprentice, not his son. But it was nice to know someone cared again and believed in me. If it hadn't been for him, I would never have had the opportunity to attend college and make something of myself." He smoothed his wrinkled jacket. "In fact, all of the clothing and possessions I took with me to school had been his, and they're the same ones I have today."

"When did he pass?" Sarah asked gently.

"While I was in medical school. He had left me his practice, but of course, I was too young to take over. So I sold the office and used the money to pay my medical school expenses. I was devastated when he died. It was a struggle adjusting after losing the kindest person I had ever known. I thought no one would ever care about me again."

"John, that's not true," Sarah insisted.

"I know," he replied and took her hand. "You care. I'm not sure why you do, but I'm glad. Don't be embarrassed about that kiss, Sarah. It meant something to me, maybe more than I thought anything ever could. I don't really know how men and women go about these things, getting to know one another better. But I do know I want to learn more about you, because you've done more than just let me know someone cares. You've made me open up my heart again so I can care too."

Chapter Nine

Sarah stood at John's side, helping him clean off the crying newborn in his arms, using the rays of morning sunlight that slowly peeked into the Pattens' cabin to guide her hand.

"Is my baby okay, doctor?" Gertie Patten asked wearily from her bed.

"So far, so good, Mrs. Patten," John replied while he continued his exam.

"Don't worry yourself into a tizzy, Gertie," Sarah told her lifelong neighbor as she walked to her bedside and wiped her flushed face with a damp cloth. "You've been through a very long and trying delivery. You need to rest."

"Oh, Sarah, I just can't rest when she's cryin' somethin' awful like that! Is she hurt?"

"No, crying is actually a good sign."

"Sarah's right," John added, "your daughter appears to be perfect, Mrs. Patten. You and your little girl are both doing very well."

"Oh, thank God," Gertie praised, smiling when John placed

the baby back into her arms. "She really is a pretty little thing, huh? I can't wait 'til Caleb sees her!"

"Well, you just rest here and I'll go get your husband for you," John offered.

"Thank ye!" Gertie called after him as he stepped out of the cabin. Nestling back against her covers, the new mother released a loud yawn. "Gosh, I'm tired. I'm so sorry Caleb had to go get you and John in the middle of the night."

"Don't be sorry, babies make their own schedules."

"Can you believe this, Sarah? I'm a ma now. Why, it feels just like yesterday that you and me was sittin' in the school-house together. You know, back then I never really did understand why you was always gone with your pa helpin' fix people up. But now that I got my little one, I know you were doin' somethin' special. Time sure flies, don't it?"

"It does," Sarah concurred.

"You wanna hold her?"

"Me?"

Gertie laughed. "Yes, of course you."

"Well, if you don't mind."

"Wouldn't have asked if I did."

Sarah gazed down at the tiny infant, feeling her heart fill with love and sadness as the little girl's cries softened when she eased her into her arms.

"We're gonna name her Meredith," Gertie said, smiling widely. "You like it?"

"It's perfect." She hugged the baby closer to her chest. "Hello, Meredith, I'm Sarah."

As she said the words, she felt a single tear trickle down her cheek. For years, she had held infants in her arms after assisting her father with deliveries and whispered an introduction. Then, it had made her happy and felt like a special gift to be able to see a newborn before anyone else in town did.

But now, Sarah longed to hold her own son or daughter in her arms. And introduce herself as a mother.

"You're real good at that," Gertie complimented. "Better than me."

Sarah rocked Meredith gently. "Don't say that. I've just held a lot of newborns."

"The way you're lookin' at her, I figure you're gonna have one of your own soon. You and that new city doctor, you are together, aren't ya?"

"We're . . . we're," Sarah hesitated, not truly knowing how to answer. Were she and John a couple now?

Suddenly, the cabin door burst open and Caleb Patten ran inside, eager to see his wife and daughter. "Gertie! Gertie, you all right?!"

"I'm fine," Gertie told him. "Tired, but fine. Don't fret about me—go meet our baby."

"Meredith," Caleb muttered, his smile growing even wider when he looked at his daughter.

Sarah extended her arms carefully. "I think she wants to meet her papa."

Speechless and awestruck, Sarah watched Caleb place gentle kisses on his daughter's face as he welcomed her into the world. Hastily, she wiped another tear, fearful as she observed Caleb and Meredith that the sadness of wanting a child of her own and her lingering grief for her father, combined with the late night, was taking its toll on her.

"Maybe we should go, John," she said briskly and turned to face him. "Now that we know Gertie and Meredith are doing well, perhaps the new family would like a little time alone."

John's brow wrinkled in concern when he looked back at her. "I think that's a fine idea," he replied. "Mr. Patten, your wife and daughter are both doing wonderfully. But if you should get worried for any reason before I come back to check on both of them tomorrow, just send word for me."

"Thank ya so much, Doc," Caleb said, offering a nod to substitute for a handshake while he held his daughter protectively. "I wish Dr. Bethel had never left us, but since he did, I reckon everyone in Templeton is lucky to have you now. Thank you for helping me beat scarlet fever so I could be here today. I know I didn't seem too grateful at the time, but I am now. You're a good man."

"You're w-welcome," John mumbled, stuttering slightly. "I'll see you tomorrow."

"Thank you too, Sarah," Caleb added. "Safe travels."

"Goodnight and congratulations," Sarah said, waving to Gertie as John escorted her out the door.

"Goodness," John whistled when they stepped into the damp morning air. "Arrive when the sun is down, leave when it's coming up."

"It certainly was a long night," Sarah agreed and released a loud yawn she was too fatigued to bother fighting. "I can't wait to go back to bed. How about you?"

"I couldn't agree more," he seconded. "I just hope that horse of yours won't be angry if we wake him to take us home."

"He'll be fine. You're not wearing one of your hats for him to knock off."

John chuckled and boosted Sarah up into the wagon. "I've finally learned my lesson." He rested a gentle hand on her shoulder after seating himself. "Are you certain you'll be able to stay awake long enough to drive us back?"

"Sure," Sarah said, yawning again. "I don't trust you to drive in these hills yet."

"Neither do I," he sheepishly confessed.

"Come on, Thunder!" Sarah called out, lightly tapping the horse with the reins. "It's time to take us back home, sweet boy."

Wearily, Thunder turned and looked back, seemingly happy when he saw Sarah and snorting bitterly after noticing John. Then he began trotting over the hills obediently.

"Are you and Gertie close?" John asked casually.

"I don't know, I guess it would depend on your personal definition," Sarah answered. "We went to school together and I've always liked her, but I don't know her nearly as well as I know May. Why do you ask? Did I seem unprofessional?"

"Oh, no, not at all. I just noticed that you had tears in your eyes when you were holding Meredith and when Caleb held her. I thought you and Gertie might have been close friends, that's all."

Sarah sighed, wishing John wouldn't have brought up her tears while her emotions were still so fresh and her fatigue was growing rapidly. "I just got caught up in the moment. Seeing a child born is a very sentimental thing."

"You don't have to defend yourself," John assured her. "I asked because when you were looking at Meredith, I saw so much love in your eyes, I would've thought she was yours. I've never seen someone look at a child who wasn't their own that way. I didn't think it was possible for you to look even more beautiful, but I was wrong."

Sarah turned her head and was automatically flustered by the loving gaze John had cast on her. "You're being far too kind," she insisted, looking straight ahead again. "But I thank you. Being a mother was something that used to be important to me."

"Used to be?"

She nodded. "I dreamed of it, just like all little girls do. But now I don't know that having children of my own will ever happen. Besides, it wouldn't be right."

"What could possibly be wrong with a woman like you having a child?"

"I'm not an ordinary woman, you've admitted that. I love the idea of being a normal woman with a family, but now that my father is gone, medicine has become just as important to me. It wouldn't be right for me to take time away from my family to go assist a doctor."

"You know, until I met you, I would've thought the same thing. But I don't think there is anything you could ever fail at, Sarah, motherhood included. Trust me, there are several children out there in the world who would adore having you as their mother."

"That's the kindest thing anyone has ever said to me," Sarah whispered, squinting when the wind blew her unruly blond waves into her eyes.

John gently tucked a few strands behind her ear. "Maybe it's something you needed to hear."

"What about you, John?" Sarah asked, growing hopeful. "Would you feel comfortable being a doctor and a father?"

"Well . . . I . . . I don't know," he stuttered. "It's really something I have never thought about, I never saw any reason to. But I guess doctors can be good fathers. Your father was, wasn't he?"

"The best," Sarah told him. "I was thinking of him tonight. He's been gone for nearly two months now, but for some reason, tonight I had almost forgotten he had passed. Deliveries were always his favorite, a nice contrast to the patients he couldn't save."

"I believe the Pattens missed him too. I imagine the entire town paid their respects at his funeral."

"Not exactly."

"What? I thought Gene Bethel was practically a saint here."

"He was. But there just wasn't time to prepare a proper funeral. After all, we were still in the middle of an epidemic. Everyone had to focus on the living, not the dead."

"That's awful," John stated wholeheartedly. "Funerals are for the living."

"It just wasn't convenient," Sarah mumbled. "You hadn't arrived yet, and I was the only one to care for the sick. I couldn't have taken time to attend a funeral. It wouldn't have been fair. I took a few moments to say goodbye the night he was buried, while most people in the schoolhouse were asleep."

"You're brave, Sarah. I took months to grieve after I lost my parents. You've barely taken a day."

She shrugged. "It's over now, I have to accept that. But I do miss him. Words can't even begin to describe it. At first, I felt so alone. Papa had always been by my side, taking me everywhere with him. People said he was crazy to have been training me in his field the way he did, but he didn't know how else to raise a daughter on his own. He couldn't teach me to knit or sew, so he taught me the only thing he could."

"And he did a fine job," John praised. "Did you do anything else together besides treating townspeople?"

"Are you always such a curious person in the early morning?"

"I was thinking about when you were asking me questions the other day, wanting to know more about what happened to make me the person I am today. And I realized there's a lot I don't know about you yet."

"I'm really not that captivating—a little boring, actually."

"Sarah, you are many things," he replied, "but one thing you aren't is boring. I wasn't kidding when I said I was going to try to open up more. I want to learn more about you and your father, because he helped you become the woman you are."

"Well, thinking back," Sarah murmured, touched by his interest, "I guess Papa and I didn't share much outside of medicine. But it didn't really matter. Even as a little girl, I knew that sharing his career with me was his way of showing me how much he loved me. I remember seeing other children whose mothers had died in childbirth with fathers who resented them, but Papa never treated me that way. He said he was glad I survived and he believed God kept my mother alive through me because I resemble her so strongly."

"Your mother must have been a very beautiful woman," John said, draping his arm around her shoulders.

Sarah was instantly comforted and warmed by his touch. Even though it was a simple gesture, she knew it didn't come easily for a man who had been as tormented as him, and that made her cherish it even more.

"Do you look like your parents?" she wondered aloud while she studied the handsome planes of his face in the early morning light.

"A little, I think. It's kind of hard to remember exactly how they looked. But I remember that my father was a tall man, with a broad chest and shoulders like mine. And I have my mother's dark blond hair."

"What did they do for a living?"

"My father worked in the stables in town and my mother worked as a seamstress."

"Stables?" Sarah chuckled. "That seems hard to believe after seeing how you and Thunder fight."

"That's because Thunder is demonic," John persisted. "And I don't have my father's touch."

"Nevertheless, I'm sure he's looking down at you now and is very proud of the doctor you've become."

"I'm sure he and my mother are proud, but not because I'm a doctor. As a child, they said all they expected from me was to grow up to be a good man. If only Caleb Patten had known how much his simple words meant."

Sarah smiled, looking up at John's sparkling eyes and complacent expression as she rested her head on his shoulder. "Maybe he did."

For a few minutes more, she kept her head down, savoring the intimate moment. She blinked and struggled to keep her eyes open when sleep began to tempt her in John's arms.

"Let me take over," he said, reaching for the reins.

"Oh, no, I can manage," she replied and began to sit up. "I shouldn't have laid my head down."

"Sleep if you like. Now that we're out of the hills, I think I can manage to get us back. That is, if my amazing teacher trusts me."

She passed over the reins. "I trust you, but I'm not sure Thunder does. Play nicely."

"You can trust me," John promised, looping his arm around her waist.

Tiredly, Sarah grinned and accepted his unspoken invitation to come closer. She placed her head on his chest, closing her eyes while she listened to his steady heartbeat. Suddenly, the tears from her dreams of motherhood and her fear of being alone were long forgotten.

She wasn't that lonely woman anymore. She was the woman in John Carson's arms.

Nervously, John paced back and forth while he waited for Sarah to arrive at the clinic. For days he had been planning a surprise for her and was far too busy to worry about her possible reaction. But now that he finally had a moment to think, all he could do was worry that the surprise he had arranged would bring Sarah more pain than comfort.

He stood when he heard a wagon pulling up and Thunder's distinctive grunting. Unable to tolerate any more waiting, he walked outside.

"Good morning," Sarah greeted cheerfully, flashing him a smile as she tied Thunder's reins to a post. "You seem to be in a hurry. Do you need to make an urgent house call? There doesn't appear to be another soul out today. We should be able to get there promptly."

"Oh, no, nothing like that. I'm just glad you're here, I wanted—" John stopped abruptly, grimacing as his hat fell into the dirt road and Thunder started smashing it with his hooves. "I forgot," he groaned.

Sarah smiled uneasily. "Sorry, John."

"It's all right," John said, casting Thunder an immature glare. "Anyway, that's really not important right now."

"You seem so somber," Sarah observed once she came closer. "Are you all right?"

"I'm fine," John promised and took her hand. "Take a walk with me?"

"Certainly."

John drew in a deep breath, tightening his grip around Sarah's fingers. He glanced at their hands, noticing how fair Sarah's skin was and how slender her fingers were compared to his. But somehow her hand fit perfectly into his, as if it had always been meant to be there.

"John, you're really worrying me. Surely you don't want to stare at my hands all day."

He placed a light kiss on her palm. "You have beautiful hands, but that wasn't my intention. I wanted you to join me at the church this morning."

"I wasn't aware of a service today, but I'd be happy to join you," Sarah replied.

"It's not a normal church service. It's something I arranged with the rest of the people in town. I only hope you won't be upset with me, and if you are, I will cancel the entire gathering immediately and you won't have to attend."

"Why don't you just tell me what it is and then let me make up my mind?" Sarah suggested gently.

"It's a service for your father, for everyone to pay their respects and remember him properly, since you were never given an opportunity to."

For a moment, Sarah stood silently, staring at him wide-eyed. John gulped nervously when he felt her fingers loosening around his hand.

"Are you all right?" he panicked. "I apologize if I've upset you. Believe me, I never intended to. You know that, don't you?"

"John," Sarah said, taking his face in her hands, "I know

that. I'm not angry. I'm just surprised—I never would've expected anyone to do this. But I'm grateful that you did. I want to be a part of this. Thank you."

"You're welcome," John said with relief and kissed her forehead. Then he walked her to the horde of people gathered outside the church, who spread through the schoolyard and into the cemetery.

"Good morning," Reverend Harrin greeted Sarah and John once he spotted them. "It looks like we're going to have to move this service outside. We can't possibly fit all of these people into the church."

"It—it looks like the entire town came," Sarah stuttered.

"I do believe they did, Sarah," the reverend agreed. "Would you like us to begin now?"

"Yes," Sarah answered with a weak nod. "We've waited far too long."

Patiently, John stood at Sarah's side, listening while Reverend Harrin supplied a prayer. Afterward, townspeople came forward, one after the other, sharing their kind memories of Dr. Bethel. Stories were told of childbirth, broken bones, scrapes and bruises, and even splinters. John listened carefully, hoping he could learn to develop a bedside manner as compassionate as Sarah's father's had been.

The service went on for hours as more stories were told. John gently rubbed Sarah's arms when the wind turned cold, trying to prove how deeply he cared for her through his actions and keep the promise he'd made to himself to try to open up again.

"And that Doc Bethel wouldn't even let me pay him," Mrs. North said, characteristically planting her hands on her hips. "Oh, but I did figure out a way to pay him by makin' him some new curtains. And the way he went on when he saw them, you'd have figured a queen made 'em. I reckon that's what I'll miss most about Gene Bethel, how polite and grateful he was. He didn't just care about the body, he cared about the soul."

After finishing her speech, Mrs. North came over, hugged Sarah, and whispered her condolences into her ear.

"Well, if everyone has spoken," Reverend Harrin announced, "I'd like to end with a prayer."

"Just a minute, preacher!" a voice called out, echoing with a country twang. "I ain't shared my story yet!"

"Hello, Pap," Reverend Harrin said knowingly to the old man as he slowly climbed up the hill. "Take your time. We're not in a hurry."

Excusing himself, John walked to Pap and held out his hand. "Let me help you up, that hill's awfully steep."

"I'm old, not dead," Pap stated bluntly. "I can make my own way up, thank ye. I don't need you helpin' me as reason to get on Sarah's good side. I know what you're up to, city feller!"

John cleared his throat awkwardly and returned to Sarah's side, feeling his cheeks burning brightly.

"Sorry I'm late, y'all," Pap apologized. "But old Lulu just didn't have any speed to her this morning. So I let the old girl mosey in nice and slow, cause it ain't right to hurry a lady, donkey or not. And then I decided to let her rest back at the general store so she didn't have to walk this hill."

Once he finally reached them, he took a few deep breaths and then respectfully removed his straw hat. "Now, let me see. Gene Bethel was a darn good man, hard to find a better one. Course, I never needed him to care for me, 'cause I don't need no doctor tendin' to me. But I liked the doc because he was so friendly to everybody. He treated everybody the same, the way a good man should. He was even nice to Lulu. I know y'all was glad to have Gene as your doctor. I was glad to have him as my friend."

"Well said, Pap," Reverend Harrin complimented, patting the scrawny man's back. "Sarah, would you like to say anything before our final prayer?"

Sarah wiped her tears. "No," she responded meekly. "I'm

afraid I wouldn't be very good with words right now. But I really do appreciate all of you coming today."

"May I say something?" John asked abruptly.

"Of course you can, son," Reverend Harrin allowed.

"Hello," John greeted the crowd uneasily. "I know I haven't had a chance to meet all of you yet, which is actually a good thing, considering if we have met you probably weren't feeling very well when we did. I know how much Gene Bethel meant to all of you, and I know that I could never replace him. But what I can promise is to be the best doctor I can be for your town and always give you the care you need. Thank you for accepting my invitation and coming here today."

Bowing his head, John took Sarah's hand as Reverend Harrin began his prayer. John's words replayed in his head: . . . *always give you the care you need.* He squeezed Sarah's hand, knowing he could keep his promise as a doctor, and praying he could keep his promise as a beau.

Sarah yawned as she descended the stairs, thankful that she had followed John's advice and rested at the clinic after the funeral service. She paused when she heard voices below. Tilting her head, she glanced down at the exam room, watching John complete an exam and stick out his tongue playfully at the little boy on the table before speaking with his mother.

She smiled, struggling to believe this was the same man who had come to Templeton with a chip on his shoulder larger than the town itself. But was it the same man?

The man she had first met would never have taken the time to plan a memorial service for a man he had never met. Nor would he have been trying so hard to become a part of her life.

She was mesmerized as she gazed at him, nearly feeling as though she was seeing him for the first time. How had John managed to transform himself so rapidly? How had he known she needed to have closure with her father's death when she hadn't even known herself?

Perhaps this was the kind-hearted, gentle man John Carson was meant to be, a man who had been buried by years of torture and heartache. This wasn't the person who had only cared about himself. This was a person who cared about people, a man who cared about her.

Quietly, Sarah sat down on the steps and observed John while he walked the young boy and his mother to the door. He knelt down, trying to make himself the same height as his tiny patient, as he praised him and offered him a piece of candy.

And in that moment, Sarah realized the feelings and attraction she had always felt for John were quickly developing into something deeper than even a courtship. But she knew John still had many more wounds to heal before he could possibly think of pursuing a relationship that led to love. Could she keep herself from falling in love with him until he was ready to reciprocate?

"Sarah!" John gasped as he turned around. "I didn't realize you had gotten up. How are you feeling?"

"Better. You were right, a nap was a good idea."

"I'm glad you heeded my advice. Sometimes emotional activities can be more draining than physical ones," John explained and offered her his hand.

"Indeed," Sarah agreed, leaning against him after he pulled her to her feet. "I saw Timmy Young was here. Is he ill or injured?"

"He's just fine." John laughed. "He and his nose just had a mishap with a piece of hay."

"A piece of hay? Congratulations, John, you are now officially a country doctor," Sarah announced. "So tell me, does it make you want to head back East?"

"No," John answered confidently, "it makes me want to stay right where I am."

"You know, there was a time I never thought I'd hear you say that."

"People change."

She smiled and gently rubbed his cheek. "Yes," she concurred, "they certainly do."

"Besides," John continued, "I had a very exciting afternoon while you slept. Patients came in and out steadily. I spent the afternoon studying warts and splinters. But if I'm being biased, Timmy was my personal highlight."

"Nothing serious, then?"

"I'm worried some people may be having complications from the scarlet fever outbreak. I believe they actually suffered side effects of rheumatic fever. I've made appointments with all of them to do extended examinations, and if necessary, I could see about making arrangements for follow-ups at a hospital in Saint Louis."

"What about you?" Sarah asked worriedly. "Shouldn't you be seen too? After all, you were very ill."

"I don't believe a trip to a hospital would provide any benefit for me."

She clutched his hand. "Why not? Don't say things like that, John, not when that illness was the reason we had a memorial service today."

John stroked her palm. "Shh. I only said it because the best medicine I've ever received is standing right in front of me."

"Do you really mean that?"

"With all my heart. Now, I think you've had enough sadness for one day. Why don't we go have some supper? Mrs. North stopped by and invited us over to the dinner party she's throwing for Ned and May in honor of their wedding next week. And Gertie and Caleb Patten will be there too, to let everyone meet little Meredith."

"That's fine, but could we wait just a moment? I have something I need to give you first."

"You don't need to give me anything."

"Yes, I do," Sarah insisted as she began searching through a cabinet. "Was Pap with Mrs. North when she came in? I'm worried about how he'll get along now that Lulu's faltering under old age. If she gets worse, he'll start walking everywhere, and we both know he can't handle that, much to his chagrin."

"Why couldn't Pap get another donkey? Keep Lulu as a pet?"

"That's what a normal person would do. This is Pap. He will not have another donkey set foot on his property until Lulu's dying day."

"We could offer to give him Thunder. A patient offered me a colt today as payment for treating his family. A *nice, friendly* colt."

"Sorry, John," Sarah told him with a grin. "I'm just as faithful as Pap."

"Figures. Do you need help looking?"

"No," she said, after spotting a small velvet box wedged into the back of the shelf, "I found it." Tenderly, she lifted the box into her hand and ran her fingertips over the smooth fabric. Without a word, she turned to John and gently pressed the gift into his hands.

John's forehead wrinkled in confusion as he opened the top and his jaw dropped when he looked inside. "Sarah," he gasped, "this—this—"

"Is my father's pocket watch," Sarah finished, smiling as she glanced at the golden circle and carved initials. "I know it can never replace your father's, but I thought it might help."

"Sarah, I appreciate this," John replied slowly, "but I can't accept it. You shouldn't part with this."

"I want you to have it," Sarah persisted. "I can't change your past, but I can give you this watch to help keep your father's memory alive, together with my father's, for the future."

"But I have nothing to give you."

"You gave me a beautiful gift today that couldn't be sealed in a box. If it hadn't been for you, my father may never have had the honorable service he deserved, and I might have continued living with a hole in my heart that I didn't know needed to be filled."

"You fill one of the holes in my heart every day. I'm just repaying that favor."

Sarah smiled and patted his jacket pocket. "Try it."

She watched silently, studying John's hands as he handled the watch delicately, turning the dial to bring the heirloom and memory of Gene Bethel back to life.

"How does it suit me?" he inquired nervously.

"Very well," Sarah complimented. "May I listen?"

"Of course," John replied and opened his arms to her.

Sarah wrapped her arms around John's waist, hugging him tightly. She shut her eyes as his lips grazed her forehead and his warm breath tickled her cheek. She listened to the rhythmic ticktock murmuring from the pocket watch, blending with his heartbeat.

Somehow John's pulse seemed stronger than it had only days before, when his heartbeat had soothed her to sleep like a gentle lullaby, as if the holes in his heart truly had been mended.

Sarah tilted her head back and looked up into his eyes, now certain she couldn't stop herself from falling in love with him. It was too late. She already had.

Chapter Ten

Johnn, do you want the medicine bottles organized in alphabetical order or by the symptoms they help treat?" Sarah asked while she dug through one of the many boxes littering the clinic floor. "John? John, are you even listening to me?"

"What—what did you say, Sarah?" John stammered and turned his gaze away from the window.

She chuckled softly. "I was asking how you would like the medicine supply organized."

"Well, just use whichever system you prefer and are accustomed to. I've used both cataloging techniques and found them to be quite satisfactory."

"Very well. Alphabetical order it is, then." She tossed a glance back at him as she filled the cabinet and arched her brow suspiciously. "You seem different today. I've never seen you so flustered before."

"Just growing impatient, I suppose. We have been cleaning and organizing the office for the last *three* hours."

"Yes, but if memory serves, it was your suggestion to start

unpacking the materials you brought from Boston as soon as it was convenient."

John nodded and sighed. "I know, I just wasn't expecting it to happen on such an exciting day."

Sarah shut the cabinet door and faced him. "I wasn't aware today was special. Is it your birthday? An important anniversary?"

"No. I was referring to the new addition outside. Come look."

She stood at his side and tilted her head. "I just see a lot of children gathered in the schoolyard. Odd that they would want to stay so late into the afternoon, isn't it? When I was their age, May and I were always eager to leave."

"Well, naturally they want to stay, Sarah. Ned Gibson and his father just installed two swings today! I'm surprised the news hadn't spread through town earlier."

"Oh, yes, Ned had mentioned he and his father wanted to set up a couple of swings for the kids before his wedding tomorrow. They thought a surprise might help bring a bit of cheer to the children after everything that happened with the epidemic, and help them see the schoolhouse and church as a peaceful place again. Hopefully the boys and girls will have a few weeks to thoroughly enjoy them before the weather turns too cold."

"Swings can be enjoyed even in the cold."

"You sound like an expert on the subject."

"I used to enjoy playing on the swings back in New England when I was a child. When I found one in a park or schoolyard that was unoccupied, I'd plop down in the seat and start pumping my legs as hard as I could. It was the most amazing feeling in the world," John recalled with a fond grin. "It made me feel like I was flying."

Sarah came closer and rested her hand on his shoulder. "It sounds nice."

John laid his hand over hers and squeezed gently. "It was

wonderful. It was one of the only ways to escape my troubles while I was awake. I'm sure it will do the same for the children in Templeton."

"And perhaps a few adults."

"That sounded quite furtive."

"It was intended be." Sarah nodded toward the window. "Look. Reverend Harrin is sending the children on their way so they can be home before the sun sets. You could take your turn."

"Sarah, I can't be seen swinging in the schoolyard! I would look foolish."

"There are worse things than looking like a fool, John." She released her hand from his and retrieved her cloak from the door hanger. "Come on."

"It's really not wise, Sarah. I'm a grown man, not a child. It couldn't possibly hold my weight."

"Yes, it can," she insisted and began guiding a jacket over his arms. "Ned and his father always try anything they put together themselves before they'll let another soul in town near it."

"Well . . . I . . . I . . ."

"Am struggling to come up with a reasonable excuse?" Sarah suggested and opened the door.

John grinned and took her outstretched hand. "Exactly. Let's go!"

With their clasped hands swaying back and forth, the couple made their way across the street to the newly vacant set of swings. John barely noticed the cool, brisk air and the dried leaves sailing in the breeze as he made his way to the schoolyard and sat down in one of the swings while Sarah took the other.

After safely securing the pocket watch Sarah had given him, that he already cherished as much as the one that had belonged to his father, he moved his feet forward and backward, slowly regaining the rhythmic pattern he had perfected during his childhood, and then started pumping his legs. He felt a rush of adrenaline course through his veins as the swing soared higher and higher. John closed his eyes and savored the feel of the wind hitting his face, disheveling his hair, and once again felt like he could fly and was free from all of life's burdens.

"Isn't it amazing to feel like this again, Sarah?"

"It must be," she replied with a smile in her voice, "you look so happy."

"Aren't you?" John pondered and opened his eyes, surprised to see Sarah sitting still. "Why don't you join in?"

"Too busy thinking, I guess. But it's a joy to watch you."

"What are you thinking about? Is something troubling you?" he asked after bringing himself to a halt.

"Oh, no, it's nothing serious, John. I was just remembering when May and I used to play out here, picking flowers and avoiding boys during recess. So many children, although they were never cruel to me, were reluctant to befriend the girl who could assist her father at such a young age. But May never seemed to mind. And tomorrow she'll be going back into the same building where we learned spelling and mathematics as children, and coming out a married lady. Time certainly does fly."

"I wish I could have known you when you were a child, Sarah."

Sarah smiled back at him. "I'm not so certain that would've been a good idea. Somehow, even as children, I could have seen us bickering."

"Despite being older than you, I admit I might have neglected to always set a good example and given in to urges to give your braids a little tug or two," John confessed and wound one of her blond waves around his finger.

"And despite the proper upbringing my father insisted upon, I might have crushed my school slate over your head occasionally in retaliation."

John grimaced. "You're right, perhaps it was for the best."

"I was only kidding. Of course I would have wanted you here and away from that horrible childhood in Boston."

Gently, John tucked the blond strand behind her ear and rested his palm on her cheek. "It's all right. Many of the days of my youth were brutal, but if I had to relive each one to be where I am today, so that I had the chance to meet you, I would."

"You don't ever have to relive those days again," Sarah whispered and leaned closer to press a soft kiss to his lips. "You're here now in Templeton where you belong."

For the first time in his adult life, John did feel as though he had perhaps found a place where he belonged and was wanted by his neighbors. But more importantly, had he also found the woman with whom he belonged? Could he one day share his life with someone else?

He returned her kiss, savoring the touch of her lips. How long could he keep Sarah satisfied with innocent kisses and hugs before she longed for a courtship with more depth that he did not yet know how to give?

"You're starting to look a little tense," Sarah commented and traced a finger over his furrowed brow. "How come?"

He shrugged. "Just remembering how different things were when I first arrived."

"Well, thanks to you, things are better now and our town is still here. The memorial you arranged for my father yesterday really gave me a bit of closure regarding everything that happened during the epidemic, and strengthened my hope that the tide truly has changed and we're entering a happier phase of life again. There's so much to enjoy. The birth of Meredith Patten, Ned and May's wedding and reception tomorrow. And, obviously, the best part is having you here to share it with."

"Well, thanks to you, I'm still here to be a part of it. And thanks to Ned Gibson and his father we have these wonderful swings to enjoy, so let's take advantage of them. I bet I can go higher than you."

"I'm positive you can," Sarah agreed. "I've never been on a swing before. Even just sitting here on a small, swaying seat feels odd. I find it kind of hard to believe you and the children enjoy it."

"You haven't been on a swing before? I just figured Ned and his father were replacing old ones."

She shook her head. "No. They're completely new and foreign to me. Ned spotted some on a trip he took to Saint Louis to look for farming supplies and was intrigued."

"Well then, I'll teach you. It's simple. Watch me. Just start moving back and forth like this," he said while providing an example, "to get a momentum going before you pump your legs."

Sarah attempted to emulate him several times, but only managed to get her shoes tangled in her long dress and make a cloud of dust that left them both coughing. She giggled lightly. "I guess this is easier for people who aren't wearing full skirts, huh?"

John laughed along with her. "It would appear that way."

"Don't let me stop you, John. Honestly, watching you is probably more fun for me than doing it myself. I like seeing you happy."

John stood and grasped the rope on each side of her swing. "I won't be happy if you're stuck sitting here while I have all the fun. I'll help you. Just keep a tight grip and don't let your hands slide or you'll get a burn."

"And you promise I'll think this is fun?" Sarah asked timidly as he pulled her back.

"Promise," he said and let go, giving soft pushes against her back each time she came closer to him. "That's good. Now, start pumping your legs. Just bend at the knee."

Sarah did as he said, struggling at first, but then she fell into a steady pattern and soared higher. "Goodness!" she exclaimed, grinning back at him while her hair flew around her face and her blue eyes sparkled wildly. "You're right! This is wonderful. It really does feel like you can fly a little!"

"I told you you'd like it."

"I love it. I've got the idea of it now. Sit back down and join me, John!"

John returned to his swing and was quickly in motion once again. But the joy of regaining the swinging sensation he had cherished in his childhood now paled in comparison to the joy that filled his heart while he watched Sarah experiencing a moment of shared happiness beside him.

"How do I look?" May asked Sarah as she pranced around the clinic, adjusting her white, lacy wedding gown. "Do I look all right? I almost feel like an intruder in your ma's fancy dress."

"You look beautiful, May," Sarah assured her. "And you're not an intruder—that dress is yours now. Just take a deep breath before you pass out."

"Pass out?"

"Just take a deep breath," Sarah repeated, smiling when May took her advice and visibly relaxed. "Better?"

"Yes." May moaned. "I can't believe I'm so nervous. All I've ever wanted is to marry Ned and now I'm shakin' like a rattlesnake. I bet Ned's standin' at the front of the church thinkin' about leavin'! We've been waitin' a good hour for Mrs. North to show up and play the organ! You think it's a sign?"

Sarah adjusted the flowers woven in May's hair. "Oh, don't be so dramatic. Ned has loved you since our childhood days. The only sign being given is proof that Pap's poor donkey is getting weaker, but your papa went out to get Mrs. North and I'm sure she'll be here any minute."

"I sure do hope things go easier for you and John when you're gettin' hitched."

"May, don't say things like that. We've barely become a couple."

"Well, that's the first step. But I knew it was only a matter of time, the whole town did. You were the only ones livin' in the dark."

Sarah blushed and awkwardly twirled the flowers in her small bouquet. "Maybe. It just feels strange to actually be part of a couple now and hear someone say my name and automatically add John's to it."

"Good strange or bad strange?"

"Good strange, if there is such a thing. It's all just happened so fast. Sometimes I even think I'm dreaming and can't possibly be feeling this way about the man who had made my blood boil when he came into town."

"You're thinkin' too much," May said simply. "Love doesn't come with a book to teach you what to do, Sarah. You've just got to let things be. And besides, you and I both know John ain't like that anymore."

Sarah grinned. "Well, sometimes he is. But now I just laugh instead of yelling at him."

"Laugh? That's it, you're in love. I knew I was in love with Ned when I just sighed instead of gripin' at him for spittin'."

"Oh, May." Sarah giggled, holding her stomach. "You're the only girl I know who could talk about spitting on her wedding day."

"Well, I'm just glad you and I actually get to be happy today."

"Of course we are. Why wouldn't we would be? This should be the happiest day of your life, May, and any tears shed are going to be happy ones."

"Oh, I know that now," May insisted. "But for a while, I thought this day was gonna be mixed with sadness because of you . . . well . . ."

"I remember," Sarah replied, recalling the conversation they'd had over a month ago before John had taken ill. "You were afraid I was going to be left all alone after you said 'I do.'"

"I sure did. But now I don't have to worry about you bein' alone, not after seein' the way John looks at you."

"It's sweet to think of me, but I won't hear of you doing it again today."

"I wish you would." May sighed and plopped down onto the examining table. "For a minute, I actually forgot about Mrs. North bein' late and—" She paused, grinning when they heard the sound of horse hooves and spinning wagon wheels outside. "Oh, maybe that's Pa! Open the door and see, Sarah!"

"I'm here, darlin's!" Mrs. North shouted as Sarah opened the door. "I'm late but I'm here!"

"And that's all that matters," Sarah insisted and stepped outside to assist May's father in helping Mrs. North out of his wagon.

"Forgive me, May," Mrs. North apologized when May hurried outside to join them, "but with Pap's donkey strugglin', I've had a mighty hard time gettin' into town."

"Don't be sorry," May said, lifting up her skirt. "I'm just glad you're here now. Let's get to the church before Ned changes his mind!"

"Now, don't everybody stand here waitin' for me," Mrs. North ordered. "You youngins go on."

"Are you sure?" May asked.

"I'll help her," Sarah volunteered, taking Mrs. North's arm. "Everyone can use an extra hand on this bumpy road."

"Oh, these old bones just don't move fast enough," Mrs. North complained. "Thank you for helpin' me, Sarah. And I'm glad to see you. I got a letter waitin' for you at the post office. I'll try to remember to get it and give it to you at the reception tonight. Someone had it sent to us from Saint Louis. You know anybody there?"

"No, I don't think so," Sarah answered, carefully walking up the church steps. "It was probably a colleague or patient of Papa's who heard of his passing and wanted to pay his respects."

"Those city folks are silly if you ask me," Mrs. North

stated as she shuffled to the organ. "Best way to pay your respect is with food, not some letter."

Sarah smiled and stifled a giggle as Mrs. North sat down and began playing the traditional wedding march. Pushing her shoulders back, she walked down the aisle slowly, glimpsing the faces of her neighbors and friends.

Ever since May asked her to be a part of her wedding, Sarah had planned to cherish each moment of her journey to the altar, believing it would be the only time she would ever follow in the same steps taken by all the other wives in town.

But now, as she watched John looking her way from the first pew, she took each step confidently and casually, no longer concerned about her future. As she reached the end, she stepped to the side and watched May enter on her father's arm.

Gently, she felt John's fingers slide over hers, as if he knew she would need the comfort of his touch to help her remember she wasn't alone when she was reminded of her own father.

Closing her eyes, Sarah bowed her head as Reverend Harrin began the service with a prayer, hoping that the next wedding she attended would be her own.

"Mmm!" John exclaimed as he weaved his way through the crowded wedding reception and seated himself beside Sarah.

"Goodness," Sarah gasped when she looked down at his filled plate. "Did you leave any cobbler or cake for anyone else?"

"A little," he answered. "Was it rude to take so much? I just can't remember ever having cobbler or cake before."

"No, it wasn't rude," Sarah replied, failing to hide the sympathy that shone in her eyes. "Eat as much as you want. I'm glad you're having a good time."

John smiled and swallowed. "A great time. I never knew wedding days could be so much fun."

"Oh, are weddings more conservative in Boston?" Sarah asked as she clapped along with the fiddlers leading the square dance.

"I wouldn't know. I've never had desserts like this or been to a wedding before."

"Never?"

"Never. I was a social outcast in Boston."

"Well, that's in the past," Sarah said firmly. "You have friends now, and a new life here."

"Yes, I do," he agreed, slipping his free hand into hers. "And much more," he added softly under his breath, afraid to let her hear. "You seem intrigued by the square dancing. Are you any good?"

"I've never tried it. I was always nervous that if I did, Papa might think I disliked the formal dances he taught me. Truthfully, I always liked them, but square dancing just looked like a lot more fun."

"It looks like an ideal opportunity to break a bone, if you ask me," John commented while he observed the couples promenading around the Gibsons' barn, stomping to the rhythm.

"I think you're just afraid to try," Sarah stated bluntly. "Worried about getting dirt on your boots, city boy?"

"Ha! Afraid? I don't think so. I played horseshoes with the other men today, didn't I?"

"Yes, and you failed miserably. And don't forget you were so far off course, you nearly hit a few innocent bystanders."

"Well, putting forth an honest effort is what really matters," John insisted, shoveling another bite of cobbler into his mouth. "And I still say Ned moved and was standing in my way. Or it was one of Thunder's old horseshoes, and therefore, under a demonic curse!"

"Oh, no." Sarah chortled and shook her head. "Now I know you're really becoming a citizen of Templeton. You're turning into a bad sport and becoming as competitive as the other men."

"I did," Sarah replied weakly as they walked to the fence. "I said he was friendly to me. . . ."

John awkwardly stuck his hand out over the fence. "Hello, horse."

Thunder neighed loudly and grunted angrily while he glared at John. He ignored John's offered petting and knocked his light blue hat off his head. Then, with pride, Thunder snorted and began stomping over the hat, digging it into the ground.

"That's what you call friendly?" John gasped. "That horse is a beast!"

"Well, look on the bright side," Sarah said as she stroked Thunder's mane, "you've finally found something you and the other men in town agree on."

"Oh, so Thunder has made it a habit of ruining their hats too? I'll have you know I really liked that hat!"

"He did you a favor. The hat was ugly as sin, John. Now do you want to see the home?"

"Eagerly," John answered, running a hand through his hair. "You don't have a 'friendly' rabid dog living in there, do you?"

"No, just a few crazed raccoons," Sarah said sarcastically as she walked over and opened the door. She sighed nervously and stepped aside. Silently, she prayed that John would be satisfied and she could control her emotions and not grow overly sentimental.

Despite her apprehension, she relaxed slightly when she breathed in the familiar scent, a combination of musk and peppermint that reminded her of her father. She scanned the open space, glancing at the wooden furniture that had been given to them as payment by a local carpenter. The thick blue curtains hanging over the windows that Mrs. North had sewn after her injured hand had been treated. New quilts made by May's mother, just before the epidemic had ravaged Templeton.

"Hardly," John replied, sipping his cider. "You won't see me spitting or chewing tobacco any time soon."

"Well, good. If you're not competitive, you won't be possessive, either, and you won't mind if I ask a gentlemen to teach me how to square dance."

"Now, hold on. I'm not possessive, but I don't think it would be fair to ask another man to teach you."

"Oh, really? And why is that?"

"Because as a beginner, you might slow him down. But don't worry. Being the gentleman that I am, I will be your partner."

"Gentlemen don't taunt ladies," Sarah reprimanded, smirking. "But don't worry. Being the lady that I am, I'll still be your partner."

Clasping hands, the couple walked toward their dancing neighbors, observing their performance before they joined.

"Oh, Sarah, John! Hold up a minute, would ya?"

John turned his head, partly disappointed and partly relieved when he saw Mrs. North slowly making her way through the crowd.

"Certainly," Sarah said. "Is everything all right, Mrs. North?"

"Nothing to complain about really," the old woman answered. "I just was needin' to speak to you, darlin'."

"Of course," Sarah replied. "How silly of me to forget. You had mentioned needing to speak with me at the church, didn't you?"

"Oh, don't you fret your pretty head with that, Sarah. I'm glad you were havin' so much fun it made you forget. You mind if we sit? These old bones of mine are givin' out after all this excitement."

"Have you been hurting long?" John asked, taking Mrs. North's arm. "Maybe you should make an appointment."

"Fiddlesticks," Mrs. North argued and shooed his hand away. "Don't you start actin' like a doctor. This is a day for celebration, not work. And we both know there's nothin' you can do to make me a spring chicken again. You stay here and watch, and make sure you learn enough that you don't step on Sarah's feet."

John smiled as he watched Sarah leading Mrs. North away, a little embarrassed to be grateful that his concern had been tossed aside. Even though tending to the sick was always his top priority, he didn't want to miss a single moment of the reception.

He wandered off a few feet outside and leaned against an old oak tree, staring back at the happy people inside the barn. Little girls and boys were giggling and dancing, trying to mirror the adults. Older townspeople were seated all around, reminiscing about their own wedding days.

"Ya know, dancin' is more fun than watchin'," a deep voice commented.

John glanced over his shoulder, surprised to see Ned Gibson standing beside him. "I guess I'll be able to determine that when my partner returns," he replied, gesturing over the hill to Sarah. "Looks like May joined Sarah and Mrs. North in their chat."

"That's how women are," Ned stated, calmly sipping his cider. "They're attracted to gabbin' like bees are to honey. Not that I mind, I was ready for a break from dancin' anyway. My feet are killin' me."

John chuckled softly. "You really have thrown a wonderful reception. Thank you for inviting me, and please accept my congratulations."

"Happy to," Ned said, shaking his hand. "But I reckon it won't be too long before I'm givin' you a handshake of congratulations."

"Why would you say that?"

"Well, you and Sarah are courtin', right? Everybody knows you only court for so long."

"Oh, I don't know about that," John told him nervously, feeling perspiration beginning to dot his forehead. "Sarah and I have only just begun courting one another, and have only known each other a matter of weeks."

"Several weeks," Ned corrected.

"All right, several," John relented. "But surely you and May courted for more than several weeks?"

"Oh, sure, we courted fer years. But I knew I'd marry May even when we was just kids. I didn't want to make her my wife until I could give us a home of our own, and she waited fer me."

"You seem calm about the idea of married life."

"Yep. What's there to be scared of?" Ned laughed. "The way I figure it, May and I made it through the fever outbreak, and that's the scariest thing we've ever dealt with. I know there will be bumps in the road, but we'll get through 'em."

John sighed, feeling envious of Ned's complacency. He turned his head, watching Sarah standing under the coming moonlight with her blond hair and lavender gown gently swaying in the breeze. How could he look at her and recognize her beauty and caring heart and not find himself wanting to marry her that very moment?

For Ned, the epidemic had been terrifying, but it had given John a sense of normalcy. He was used to treating the sick and dealing with the unexpected. What he wasn't used to were the simple, normal things that most people took for granted and never feared, the things that he and Sarah would face as their relationship grew.

John ran his hands through his hair anxiously, feeling torn between the tormented young boy and the belittled, angry man he had been. He looked around the reception at his neighbors and friends, wondering if he could ever truly become one of them or if he would always be the man who was stuck somewhere in between.

"Hey, you ladies all right?" he heard Ned ask when Sarah and May returned. "I've never seen two people look so sad at a weddin'."

John lifted his head, startled by Sarah's solemn expression as she stood before him, gripping an envelope in her trembling hands. "Sarah, is everything all right? Did you receive some bad news?"

"Yes—" May began, stopping suddenly once Sarah shook her head.

"Stop, May, now don't you forget that you promised we weren't going to talk about this now," Sarah said calmly and slid the letter into her pocket. "It's silly of me to get flustered over a letter of condolence about my father when I'm at such a wonderful party."

"Is that all?" John questioned, exchanging worried glances with Ned.

"Not exactly," Sarah murmured. "Mrs. North is quite concerned about Pap, since she hasn't been able to see him very much because of Lulu's health. And May and I were just upset that Pap couldn't be here with us. We all think of him as family."

"Yes, indeed," Ned agreed with a nod.

"Anyway," Sarah said, regaining her composure, "I promised you and I would ride out to Pap's tomorrow to visit. Is that all right?"

"Certainly," John said.

"Great. Now that that's all settled, I do believe you owe me a dance, Dr. Carson."

"Yes, Miss Bethel, I believe I do."

"Then let's go!" Sarah exclaimed, running ahead of him when a new song started.

"Wait for me, Sarah!" John hollered after her, grasping her hand as he trailed behind. "Please wait for me to catch up," he added, thankful that she didn't know the truth hidden behind his simple request.

Chapter Eleven

Sarah, are you sure we're going the right way?" John asked as he guided the wagon over sloping, deep hills and gazed at the endless fields and trees that surrounded them. "I'm not sure we're even in Missouri anymore, let alone Templeton."

"Just keep going," Sarah insisted. "You weren't expecting Pap to live within the town limits, were you?"

"No," John admitted, "but I was expecting him to live in the same country. It seems odd to me that such a giving man who always wants to help people lives so far away from all of them."

"Pap grew up in these hills, before Templeton even existed—he'd never abandon them. But I packed a picnic for us, if you would like to stop."

"How did you know I was getting hungry?"

"Because every time Thunder gets this far, he begins to get cranky and needs an apple or carrot to encourage him to keep going."

John grimaced and glanced down at the grunting horse. "I think he's as insulted as I am."

"Insulted or not, you're both male. And I've learned that most men are happier with a full stomach."

"Well, I can't very well argue with basic anatomy," John grumbled as he gently brought the wagon to a stop. "But I bet if I compared you to Pap's donkey, just because you're both female, you wouldn't take it very well."

"Why wouldn't I?" Sarah asked, crossing her arms. "She's gentle and until her body started giving out, she was a hard worker. As long as you don't say I look like her, I don't have a problem with the comparison."

"You know," John said while he climbed down and assisted Sarah, "I'm beginning to think I'll never win an argument with you."

Sarah walked over to an open spot of grass and set their picnic basket on the ground. "And I'm beginning to think you'll never have enough sense to remember that and quit encouraging them."

"I enjoy annoying you too much to stop."

Smirking, Sarah knelt down on the grass, unwilling to admit she also enjoyed their bickering, and remembering how they had argued so childishly when they'd first met.

"So, what's for lunch?" John asked as he began unpacking their meal.

"Well, there's some bread and applesauce Mrs. North gave me." Sarah paused and gulped, looking at John nervously when he got to the bottom of the basket. "And there's also—"

"Pie!" John exclaimed when he pulled out the pan. "Do you mind if we start with dessert first? It looks great."

"Looks can be deceiving," Sarah whispered.

"Don't be silly. After the wedding reception yesterday, I doubt a bad pie exists," John proclaimed and took a large bite.

Suddenly, his smile faded and his eyes watered. He grimaced and roughly swallowed, pushing the pie away. "I stand corrected," he gasped, quickly sipping from the water canteen Sarah handed him.

"Well, at least now you know my secret," Sarah mumbled.

"You made that?" John asked sheepishly.

"Yes. I'm sorry! I really tried this time to make it correctly, but it still turned out horribly. But now you know that I'm not capable of making more than boiled eggs or heating an already-prepared meal over a fire. Are you upset?"

"Upset?" John repeated, arching his brow. "Why would I be upset? It's just a pie, Sarah."

"Not to some men," she told him somberly. "Most men expect a woman to be a good cook and do not even want to court her if she's not. My father may have taught me how to stitch wounds and treat illnesses, but cooking wasn't something he was a master at."

Gingerly, John reached out and cradled her face in his hands. "Sarah, by now you should know that I do not have much in common with a lot of men here. Why should I care if you can cook? That has nothing to do with your heart and your spirit, and that's all I really care about. And actually, I find it rather funny that you and I can end a scarlet fever epidemic, but I struggle with simple things like wagons and horses and you struggle with cooking."

Sarah smiled back at him. "I guess it is a little funny."

John brushed his lips across her forehead. "Don't be worried. Besides, I can actually cook a little."

"Really?"

He nodded. "I had to cook for the awful family I was a servant for. Maybe I can help you."

"I'd like that," Sarah admitted.

"Good. But if it's all the same to you, I think we should stick to Mrs. North's cooking for now."

"I couldn't agree with you more."

"And speaking of Mrs. North, you seemed awfully upset

yesterday after she gave you that letter. I didn't want to press the issue because of the wedding, but I was curious to know if everything was all right."

"The letter was from my uncle," Sarah answered slowly. "I was just upset to be reminded of my father's death on such a happy day."

"Did he say anything important?"

Sarah shrugged. "He passed on his condolences."

"That's all?"

"Basically." She paused and took a breath. "Telegrams don't leave much room for details, not that I should expect any. I've never even met him, but he did say he was sending a letter later."

"Perhaps he intends to invite you to come visit him."

"Maybe, but it would be very difficult. Going to New York would be a very long and expensive journey that I'm not certain I'd like to attempt."

"New York?" John repeated. "No wonder you don't seem eager to go."

"Why would you say that?"

"Because I know how much you love Templeton, even if you do not have much in common with your neighbors. I can't imagine you ever wanting to leave."

"I do love this place and am not eager to go so far away, but I wouldn't mind a little travel. In fact, I had been trying to find the courage to ask Papa to allow me to accompany him to Saint Louis the next time he went."

"Ah, were you wanting to experience shopping in a city with more than a general store?"

"No, I wanted to actually go inside a library. I've been fortunate to read many novels, but only ones I got from teachers or through a catalog at the general store. I thought it would be exciting to go inside one place and have so many stories to pick from without needing to pay or wait to dive into the pages."

"Well, perhaps you could still go. I'd like to go to Saint Louis occasionally, to meet with other doctors to stay up-to-date with the medical world. You should come with me. Maybe you'll even inspire me to pick up a novel. I've been reading medical books and studies for so long I had actually forgotten that some people read for pleasure. So, what's your favorite book?"

"The Swiss Family Robinson."

"Really?"

"Yes, really. Why do you look so surprised? Did you assume it would be a romance simply because I'm a girl?"

"No, I learned a long time ago you're not a typical girl— it's part of the reason I like you so much. I just figured your favorite would be a mystery, since you took such an interest in my past."

"I like a good mystery," Sarah admitted, "but getting to know more about you is better than any book filled with fictional characters."

"Then I guess it's about time I start learning more about you," John retorted easily.

"You know quite a bit."

"Yes, I guess I do, but there's still more I'd like to know. The simple, little things I've never known about someone before because I never had the chance to get that close to them. Would you mind answering a few questions?"

Sarah grinned and curled up beside John. "No, but you have to promise to tell me your answers to the questions too."

"Deal," John agreed as he wrapped his arms around her. "Um . . . What's your favorite color? I like blue, personally."

"Lavender."

"What's your favorite time of day?"

"Dawn."

"Mine's dusk. Hmm . . ." John hummed while he searched for another question. "How about your favorite animal?"

"Thunder, naturally." Sarah giggled. "But I'm guessing you'll have a different answer."

Amy Blizzard

"Why don't you ask me a question?" John suggested, smirking.

"All right," Sarah said, pausing briefly. "What's your favorite moment?"

"I don't know, it's hard to pick one. . . . But I do know this one is pretty special. I know you want to go and see Pap, but do you think we could stay here a few minutes longer?"

Sarah rested her head on his shoulder. "Of course we can, if you want to."

"It's just so nice," John commented softly as he ran his fingers through her hair. "In the city it's practically impossible to have a moment like this, that's so quiet, personal, and simple."

Sarah hugged John tightly, barely hearing him murmur "How could I have been afraid of this?" under his breath over the ticking of her father's pocket watch. She glanced into his dark eyes, which were now sparkling and vibrant and hardly contained any of the coldness or anger he had come to Templeton with.

As she sat with him, she felt so tempted to whisper "I love you" into his ear and finally confess the feelings she was keeping inside. But she knew that the timing was not yet right and John still had a lot of trusting and learning to do before he could love her in return.

But now she knew more than ever that he was keeping his promise to become a better man, and one day soon, she would look into his eyes and see only love in them. Then she would share with him the three most sacred, heartfelt words one person could say to another.

"Well, here we are," Sarah announced as they passed in front of a rundown, old log cabin.

John jumped out of the wagon and stretched his legs. "I don't know how Pap manages to make that long drive so often. I think my train ride from Boston may have been shorter."

"Yes, it's definitely a lengthy trip," Sarah agreed as he lifted her down.

"But I'm sure it will be worth it."

"John, wait," Sarah whispered before they walked to the door. "Before you go in, I just wanted to ask if you were hungry."

"No, of course not, after the picnic you packed."

"Good."

"Why on earth would you ask that?"

Sarah blushed. "The long drive isn't the only reason I always pack a picnic when I come out here. My cooking is pretty bad, but not quite as awful as Pap's possum porridge."

"Possum?" John mumbled, grimacing. "Suddenly I don't think I'll ever be hungry again."

"I'm sure you'll change your mind the next time you smell Mrs. North's bread or pies," Sarah commented as she reached the door.

John stood patiently in Pap's yard while Sarah knocked, glancing at the empty buckets in the donkey's pen that were obviously intended to hold food and water, and the broken cabinets and wagon wheels that were lying around in need of mending. Rapidly, a sour feeling spread through his stomach as he thought of the friendly, giving old man he had come to know. He could never imagine Pap sleeping in on a Sunday afternoon, allowing his donkey to go hungry and thirsty and his neighbors' possessions to go unattended.

Quietly, he walked around the corner and peered inside through a cracked window. His eyes widened when he saw a shadowed, unmoving figure lying in bed, completely oblivious to Sarah's knocking.

"That's odd," Sarah said after she knocked once more. "Pap normally answers quickly and is always excited to have company."

"Um, why don't you go get Lulu some water?" John

suggested calmly. "I'll try knocking. Maybe I can be louder than you," he rambled, hoping he could spare Sarah any pain or shock, if possible.

"All right," Sarah agreed uneasily.

Once Sarah had turned away, John looked over his shoulder and hurriedly pushed open Pap's unlocked door. He rushed to the old man's bedside and removed the blankets covering him.

"C'mon, Pap, wake up!" he begged as he flipped him onto his back. "Pap, can you hear—" John paused abruptly when he saw Pap's ashen face lying limply on his pillow.

With a heavy heart, he pressed his fingertips to Pap's neck and wrist, searching for a pulse. Then he rested his ear to his chest.

"John!" Sarah screamed from the doorway, her footsteps echoing loudly in the eerie silence when she ran to the bed. "John, what's wrong? Is he sick? How can I help?"

John lifted his head and faced her with a heavy heart. "You can't help him, Sarah. He's gone."

Chapter Twelve

Numbly, Sarah walked hand in hand with John to the clinic, shivering at the sound of her neighbors singing hymns as they began their journey back home after Pap's funeral.

"Sarah, are you all right?" John asked. "I don't think you've said a word all day."

"I'm just . . . stunned," she admitted. "I know Pap was old, but I just never imagined he would be gone so suddenly, especially after avoiding illness during the scarlet fever outbreak. He had been looking tired from walking more because of Lulu's atrophy, but—"

"Stop, darling," John interjected, "it won't do any good to dwell on this. Pap was an old man. Most likely his heart just gave out in his sleep."

Sarah sniffled. "It seems hard to fathom a heart as big and as good as his could just give out. I thought the funeral would last into the night, once everyone in town started sharing their fond memories of him. He helped anyone and everyone."

John smiled back at her. "Even city fellers like me."

"And apparently he rubbed off on you," she commented once they reached the clinic where Thunder and Lulu were tied to posts outside. "I can't believe you agreed to take Lulu in."

"Well, according to Pap, it's improper to forget her name or even rush her," John recalled as he stroked one of the donkey's ears. "So I can only imagine how heartbroken he would be if she were without a home. Besides, it's not like she has an obsession with ruining my hats."

Halfheartedly, Thunder reached out with his snout and pushed the black hat from John's head, but refrained from stomping on it.

"I know, Thunder," Sarah murmured and patted his mane, "you miss him too."

"Come on, Sarah," John said after he unlocked the clinic door, "let's get out of the chilly air."

Sarah followed slowly and shut the door behind her. But while John started a fire, she could not bring herself to walk away from the window. She stood frozen, staring into the distance at the graveyard just beyond the church.

John stepped up behind her, gently unbuckled her black cloak, and removed it from her shoulders. "You should come away from the window and have a seat by the fire to warm yourself."

"It feels wrong to turn away. Will this ever stop, John?" Sarah wondered innocently. "First the epidemic took so many lives, and then Pap went suddenly. Are any of our lives safe?"

He took her arm and led her to a chair. "Sarah, you're worrying too much. Outbreaks happen and take lives. Pap died because he was old and ready. But you and I are fine, and we're going to stay that way for a long time."

"You can't be certain of that. Are you forgetting that you almost died?"

"Of course not, but always worrying about death would

defeat the purpose of having my life spared. Has something happened to make you worry?"

"I'm fine. It's just impossible not to think about death and how suddenly things can change after everything that's happened. Within months, I lost my father, lifelong neighbors, and now dear old Pap. I used think about the future, knowing how important it is to be patient and wait for things to happen as they naturally should. But now the future seems so uncertain. It feels like things should be said and done in the present before it's too late."

"Maybe you're right," John replied casually. "I've seen patients have a brush with death and want to try things they never would have before. I saw a young man stand up to his father and tell him he didn't want to join the family business after surviving a terrible fall. Is there something you want to do?"

"Not exactly," Sarah murmured. "But there is something I've wanted to say that I originally thought should wait."

John smiled and gave a mild chuckle. "Is that all? Well, go ahead and tell whomever it is what you have to say."

"Even if it's you?"

"Of course. Sarah, what's got you so flustered?"

"You," she answered lightly when he sat down beside her. "The past several weeks with you have been a whirlwind. When you first came here with your façade of regal ways, I never would have thought you would change my life, but you did. As I watched you revealing more of who you really are every day, I realized I was growing and changing with you, because you were becoming a part of me."

"I'm not sure what to say," John stammered. "I was the one who needed to change. You were fine the way you were."

"That's what I thought too, but I was wrong, because I'm happier with you here."

"Well, I'm happier now too," he mumbled awkwardly, "but I don't see why that's anything to get flustered about."

"John," Sarah whispered through a smile, "I don't think you understand what I'm trying to tell you." She paused and took his hands. "John, I love you."

John sat silently for several moments and felt his hands involuntarily go limp in Sarah's firm grip. Guilt washed over him when he glanced into her eyes, knowing he should say something in return.

Telling Sarah he loved her should have come naturally; any man should have felt honored to have her love. But he did not feel honored or even happy. He felt scared. After years of being an unwanted child tossed into asylums and filthy homes, he had forgotten what love was and how to receive it and give it in return.

"Aren't you going to say anything?" Sarah murmured into his ear.

"W-well," he stuttered, loudly clearing his throat. "Thank you."

Sarah laughed and rubbed his tense shoulders. "Relax. It's all right if you're not ready to say it back. I know it may sound sudden. I wasn't planning on telling you how I felt for a long time. But after losing Pap without any warning, I thought it was important to tell you now while I still had the chance. I know opening up isn't easy for you and I understand if you need more time."

"Sarah, I know you're compassionate, but are you sure you can understand?" John wondered tiredly. "What if I'm never ready? Will you be able to understand that?"

"What are you talking about?"

"Love." John sighed and reluctantly pulled away from her. "I'm not like you. Even when your mother died, you had your father to love you. When he died, you were surrounded by a town that adores you. When my parents died, I was thrown into an asylum filled with sick and crazy people."

"That was years ago. All of those people are out of your

life now and you're surrounded by the same kind neighbors I am. That life is over. Why don't you start a new one?"

"Because it's not that easy!" John cried in exasperation as he walked to the window, staring outside blankly, unable to face her.

"What is wrong with you?" Sarah questioned, dumbfounded. "Why are you getting upset with me for loving you?"

"Because I'm mad at myself," he said angrily. "I never should have allowed myself to open up to you and care about you the way I do, knowing I could probably never return your love if I was ever lucky enough to earn it."

Awkward, silent moments passed before Sarah spoke quietly. "That is the cruelest thing anyone has ever said to me."

"What?" John gasped, startled by the tears glistening in Sarah's eyes when he turned around to face her. "I'm not mad at you, I'm mad at myself."

"But you regret allowing yourself to care for me," Sarah mumbled back, blinking to allow her tears to flow freely.

"I didn't mean it like that!" He reached out to wipe away her tears, heartbroken when she reeled away. "I don't regret caring about you. I just regret earning your love when I don't know if I can ever return it. Maybe I'm just incapable of it."

"You don't know that, John. All of that pain that is stifling you is in the past. You have a future that can be different, if you want it to be. How can you be so certain you'll never be able to love someone?"

"It's been years and years and I'm still haunted by the memories. If my troubles haven't ended completely by now, they never will."

Sarah gritted her teeth and shook her head angrily. "No, of course they won't, because you don't want them to!"

"Y-you think I want to be like this?" John sputtered out.

"Yes!" she cried. "For many years you were surrounded by people who didn't love you, John, and I know you can't help that. But now you're pushing away someone who does love you and hurting yourself. It was foolish of me to believe you could love me one day when you won't even let anyone love you."

"That's crazy," John hissed as he paced back and forth, clenching his fists. "You really think I want to be like this?"

"Yes, I do," Sarah answered clearly. "Because if you keep yourself hidden in your past, you have an excuse not to try to fight to build a better future. You can stay locked away, never letting anyone in and never risk being hurt again."

John glared back at her while he struggled to catch his breath. "That's not true," he denied aggressively. "I have tried. I opened up to you. I told you about my history and learned about yours. I'm a better doctor now and a better neighbor than when I came here. And for the first time in my life, I cared about someone. I care about *you!*"

"But that's all you're willing to do," she retorted evenly. "You're only willing to care."

Exasperated, he asked, "Why isn't that enough?"

"Because I deserve more!" Sarah shouted.

John smiled back at her weakly. "Well, I guess we finally found something we agree on. You *do* deserve more. Maybe you should move on, find someone better."

"Maybe you're right." Her strong voice fell hoarse and meek. "Too bad you're the only man I've ever wanted to be a part of my life. But I should thank you for letting me know that we could never build a life together while I still have other options in other places."

"What other options in other places?"

"I received the letter my uncle had mentioned in his telegram. He's offered to let me come stay with his family in New York. Perhaps it would be best if I accepted his offer."

"Sarah, don't be rash," John said. "Maybe you are related through blood, but you know your real family's right here. Besides, you would be bored in New York. The doctors there won't care if you are a doctor's daughter. None of them would ever let you assist them. Do you really think you could be happy living with strangers, unable to help anyone? We both know you thrive on helping others."

"I will be helping others," she declared. "In exchange for room and board, my uncle has requested I act as a nanny to his young children and assist with the cooking and cleaning as needed."

John rolled his eyes. "He doesn't want to help you—he wants you to help *him*. He doesn't want you to come because he wants to meet his niece, he just wants a servant! Trust me, I've been there and I don't want to see that happen to you."

"Even if that is the truth, I won't be living in the same horrid conditions that you did. And what I decide to do shouldn't concern you, anyway."

"It concerns me because I care about you," he said wholeheartedly.

"And I love you," Sarah reminded him. "But there isn't any point in spending time with you, being part of a courtship that will never go anywhere."

"Then let me leave," John offered. "I'll send word to Boston that you need another doctor and stay until one comes. I'll even see to it that he allows you to be a part of his practice and he lives in the spare room upstairs, so you can keep the house."

"No, people here trust you now and you're finally building a home for yourself. I wouldn't take that away from you or my friends. I'll be fine in New York."

"You sound like you have already made up your mind."

"I guess I have."

"I can't believe you're willing to leave the only home you've ever known, just because I can't tell you I love you," John told her honestly. "I never thought such a strong woman would act so childishly."

"And I never thought a grown man would act so angrily

when he learned someone loved him," she replied coolly. "I know you've had a rough life, but mine hasn't been easy lately, either. I can handle waking up every day, knowing I will never see my father again, but seeing you as you are now, instead of the man I learned to love, is more than I can take. Thunder and I are going back to the house to enjoy what time I have left there. My uncle will be expecting me in a few weeks. Goodbye, John, and good luck."

"Wait," John whispered as Sarah opened the door, heart-broken by the pleading look she gave him when she paused in the doorway, knowing she desperately wanted him to give her a reason to stay. "Your father's pocket watch," he said, and fumbled to remove it from his jacket. "You should take it with you."

"Keep it," Sarah insisted as she wrapped a shawl over her head and shoulders. "It was a gift, and even if you don't want it, it's something *I* want you to have."

John gripped the watch and held it to his chest while he watched Sarah slip out the door, feeling his heart break as he let the woman who had saved his life walk out of it.

Chapter Thirteen

Quit bein' so silent, Doc, you're makin' me nervous. Don't be scared, just tell me straight. I need to know what's been makin' me feel so poorly, no matter how bad it is."

John sighed as he glanced up at Mrs. North and removed the stethoscope from her chest. "Well," he murmured, "this is a diagnosis I've never had to give before in my practice. To be honest, Mrs. North, at one time I actually didn't even believe in it."

"It's that bad?"

"Yes and no. Technically, you're healthy. I believe your symptoms are being caused by a broken heart."

"A broken heart," Mrs. North echoed. "You know, only days ago I would've told you that you were silly in the head, but now I know you're right. When Pap Dickens was around, I never wanted to admit just how much that old man meant to me, but now that he's gone, I almost feel lost without him. You got any idea what the cure is for this sadness?"

"No, I'm afraid I don't have any medicine in the clinic that could help cure you. But I can offer you my advice. I may not have had the pleasure of knowing Pap as long as you did, but I don't think the man I met would want you to be so upset and forlorn. After all, Pap's greatest joy in life was helping others and making them happy."

"You're right, but I can't seem to make myself cheer up just the same. But you of all people should know how that feels."

John cleared his throat, turned away, and walked across the room to organize medicine bottles to busy himself. "I'm sorry. I really don't know what you're talking about."

"Oh, fiddlesticks you don't know what I'm talkin' about!" Mrs. North argued as she pushed herself off the exam table. "I see those dark circles under your eyes because you ain't had any sleep in days. You've got the same sad look I see on my face every time I look at my reflection. You miss Sarah."

"Of course I do," he answered steadily. "She was a dear friend and a very intelligent woman, who helped with my practice here."

"Enough of your smart talk and stale answers," Mrs. North grumbled, rolling her eyes. "It ain't right to talk about Sarah like she was just your friend and nurse. She was the woman that saved your life in more ways than one. That girl loves you."

John shut his eyes and wished he could block out Mrs. North's words. He didn't need to be reminded that Sarah loved him. Ever since she had uttered those three precious words to him, he hadn't been able to forget them or his ridiculous response. And he still struggled to understand how she had managed to fall in love with someone as undeserving as he was to begin with.

"It's really very kind of you to be concerned, Mrs. North, but it's far more paramount that we focus on you than me."

"Not really," she debated. "We both know I can't go back and tell Pap how I really felt about him, to try to mend my broken heart. But you still have a chance to mend yours, and Sarah's as well. How could you let her go to Saint Louis this morning? Why didn't you try to stop her?"

"Sarah has already made her decision. And I never said I loved her!" John exclaimed, shaking his head.

"You don't have to, some things are just plain. And frankly, if you don't love her, you're a fool, boy. You'd be hard-pressed to ever find another girl as beautiful or intelligent. But most importantly, you'd never find someone that cares about you the way she does."

"You're right," John confessed defenselessly, remembering how Sarah had been the first person to ever want to learn more about him and help him heal from his broken past. She had even saved his life when he contracted scarlet fever. "Mrs. North, I—I want to love Sarah, but I don't really know what love feels like."

"Darlin', love isn't somethin' you can learn about in your doctor books, it's something you gotta' feel. How do you feel when you think about Sarah?"

"Happy and comforted," he responded with ease. "I think about her, and all of sudden, I can hear the sound of her voice and the feel of her touch, even if she's not there . . . because it's become such a part of me."

Mrs. North smiled and grasped his hands. "If that's not love, I don't know what is. Now what are you gonna do to try to stop that love from slippin' away?"

"You don't have to go, Sarah!" May persisted, pacing back and forth in front of the train station while Sarah unloaded her belongings from Ned's wagon.

"May," Sarah whispered, "I wouldn't have troubled Ned to drive me all the way to Saint Louis if I thought I might change my mind. Going to New York is best."

"It wasn't any trouble," Ned said as he lifted down a trunk.

"And I'd be just as happy to take you back to Templeton with us. You don't know how hard this new wife of mine is gonna be to live with after you leave."

"You'll be fine, you have each other," Sarah reminded them and forced herself to smile.

"And who will you have?" May asked worriedly.

"A family. I'm going to stay with my uncle."

"Humph!" May grunted, crossing her arms. "I'd hardly call that family. John was right, he ain't wantin' you to come and be his niece, he wants you to be a servant!"

"I'd be acting as a nanny, not an overworked maid."

"But what about helpin' people the way you used to with your pa? How can you walk away from the only life you've ever known? You still have places to go—you can stay with me and Ned or Mrs. North."

"I know that," Sarah said tearfully, "but I just can't, May. I can't stay and be reminded of John and all of the sadness that's plagued Templeton. I think I need to make a new life for myself."

"But what if that new life ain't worth having?"

Sarah shut her eyes and wished May would stop providing so many logical reasons for her to stay. Even though her confrontation with John had happened nearly two weeks ago, she hadn't been able to forget it. Was John right? Was she acting too hastily by packing her bags and leaving Templeton to go live and work for strangers just because he could not return her love?

"I've made my choice, May, and if I made the wrong decision, I'll just have to accept the consequences."

"Oh, blast John Carson!" May grumbled.

"May!" Sarah gasped. "You shouldn't speak that way."

"Maybe I should," she argued. "Because before John Carson showed up, my best friend would never be doin' somethin' so crazy! If he hadn't come and you hadn't fallen for him, you wouldn't be leavin' now."

Sarah sighed, unable to argue with the truth, but also knowing she would never trade falling in love with John, even if she could have known how horribly everything would turn out in the end.

"That's what this is about?" Ned asked and scratched his head. "You're leaving because you and the doc had a quarrel?"

"It was more than a quarrel," Sarah clarified. "John and I had been having quarrels since the day we met. I can handle that and even laugh it off later. But I can't handle knowing that John isn't sure he'll ever be capable of returning someone's love."

"Doesn't know?" Ned repeated. "Seems kinda dumb fer him to be sayin' that, considerin' he loves you."

"No, he doesn't, Ned. If he did, he would have told me."

"Well, maybe he didn't tell ya, but I thought he was tryin' to show ya."

"How?" May grunted. "By bein' as cold as ice in winter?"

"No, by doin' nice things. He gave her pa the funeral he deserved, so she could say goodbye the right way. He was willin' to let her have the house when she wanted to stay. And he's just got to be in love, because he's agreed to let Thunder stay with him and Lulu after Sarah moves. Only a crazy man would agree to tend that riled-up horse—or a man that's in love. And other than wearin' some ugly hats and suits, the doc don't seem crazy."

"Well," May said as she chewed on her bottom lip, "Ned does have a point. Besides, Ned don't tell me he loves me a lot in words, but I know that he does."

"Of course he does. But Ned was never afraid of commitment, May," Sarah reminded her. "The only reason you had a long engagement was because he wanted to be able to give you a stable life when you became his wife. And everything John did for me was very nice, but it doesn't change anything. If he did love me or thought he would be able to someday, he had two weeks to tell me and give me a reason to stay, and he never did."

"All aboard!" the train conductor shouted suddenly, waving toward the waiting passengers. "Boarding for Chicago, Illinois!"

"That's me," Sarah whispered.

"Are you sure?" May questioned. "He said Illinois. You're headin' to New York."

"I have a few transfers before I get there."

"Well, I guess now there's no talkin' you out of it," Ned said matter-of-factly and began gathering her luggage. "I'll get this stuff on the train so you ladies can have a few extra minutes."

"Oh, Sarah!" May cried. "This ain't right. I'm gonna be lost without you."

"No you won't," Sarah replied, trying to push away her own tears. "You're a newlywed with a wonderful life ahead of you and a husband who loves you very much."

"I know." May sniffled. "But just because a gal is married doesn't mean she doesn't need friends, especially a best friend."

"We'll still be best friends," Sarah promised as she hugged May and let her own tears fall. "Even if we're miles apart, it doesn't mean our friendship has to stop. We can write letters. And that will give me something to look forward to whenever I get homesick."

May nodded. "All—all right," she gasped, struggling to speak, "I'll write. My letters won't be fancy like yours, but I'll do my best to make them nice."

"All aboard!" the conductor shouted once more.

"I guess I better go," Sarah mumbled and slowly pulled herself out of May's embrace.

"Your stuff's all loaded," Ned announced when he returned.

Sarah reached out and squeezed his hand. "Thank you, Ned. Thank you for all your help."

"Anytime," he said and planted a quick kiss on her cheek. "And remember, you always have a place with me and May in case New York life don't suit you."

"I will," she promised. "Goodbye."

Sarah hurried off and joined the other passengers lined up beside the train. She kept turning her head to glance at May, wanting to look at her for as long as she possibly could, knowing very well this could be the last time she would see her best friend.

The line moved steadily, and within minutes it was her turn to board. She climbed onto the steps and paused when she saw May crying into Ned's shoulder. "Oh, Lord," she prayed quietly and closed her eyes, "please give me a sign to let me know if I'm doing the right thing."

Sarah gasped and opened her eyes when she thought she heard someone calling her name. She stared ahead, startled to see a huge cloud of dust forming in the distance, surrounding a horse.

"Sarah!" May exclaimed. She squinted to try to view the figure. "Is that John?"

"Riding Th-Thunder," Ned stammered, shaking his head in disbelief when John Carson came closer, hanging over sideways on the horse's back. "What man in his right mind would ride Thunder? Heck, maybe he *is* crazy!"

"I didn't know John could ride a horse. He couldn't even drive a wagon," Sarah said as she stepped off the platform.

"He ain't ridin'," Ned said bluntly. "He's hangin' on fer dear life!"

"Sarah! Sarah, wait!" John implored once Thunder reached the train station and practically dumped him onto the ground. "I have to talk to you!"

"Oh, Thunder!" Sarah whispered through a smile as she and Ned grabbed his reins and helped settle him down. "Thunder actually let you ride him? I didn't know you could ride a horse."

"Neither did I," John panted as he struggled to catch his breath. "But there's a first time for everything, and after I let him stomp on a few of my hats, he let me climb on his back."

Sarah stared up at John in utter shock while she patted Thunder. "Are you crazy? You could have gotten yourself killed! Thunder could have been hurt! What on earth possessed you to ride on horseback all the way to Saint Louis?"

"You," John answered simply when his breathing returned to normal. "You did. I had to see you again before it was too late. I'm sorry. I'm so sorry, Sarah."

"Don't bother apologizing. Everything has already been said and done. It's over," Sarah murmured, wishing she could believe herself. As she gazed up at John, she fought to not reach up and brush away the dust that was smudged on his face and hair so she could touch him one last time.

"Miss!" the conductor yelled from the train. "Do you plan to board or not?"

John gently grasped her arms. "Wait, Sarah, please. Just hear me out. And then, if you still want to go, I won't stop you again."

"May I have a minute? Please?" Sarah asked the conductor, glancing back at him pleadingly.

"Oh . . . well . . ." the conductor groaned with an agitated sigh. "All right, one minute, but only one."

"Come back, Sarah," John whispered into her ear, "you don't want to do this, I know you don't. Your home is back in Templeton. You don't want to leave Mrs. North and May and Ned, all your friends. And even Thunder. Everyone knows you love him."

Sarah stood silently and stared at the ground, unable to look into his eyes. Why was he reminding her of everything she already knew? Why couldn't he say the one thing that would make her stay?

"And me," John said loudly, practically allowing the entire station to hear. "Stay for me. I know I may not deserve to have you in my life, but even if I don't, I still want you to be a part of it, because I won't have a home until I have you."

"What? John, you're not making sense. You once told me all you really wanted was a house of your own and a chance to leave Boston. You have a home now."

"No, no, I don't," he persisted. "I don't want your house, Sarah, or Templeton, because it doesn't matter if you're not there. You were right—I do need to forget my past. Because if I had just opened my eyes, I would have seen that everything I ever dreamed of wanting was right in front of me.

"I wanted more than a house. I wanted a home," John elaborated as he gingerly placed his hands on Sarah's shoulders and stared into her eyes. "You're my home, Sarah, and I won't be happy anywhere unless you're with me. Because as long as I have you, I'll have everything I need. No one could blame you if you still wanted to go, not even me. But I'm begging you not to. Please come back to Templeton with me and help turn that lonely house into a home."

"I—I," Sarah stammered, turning away briefly when the train conductor tapped her shoulder.

"Going or staying?" he asked tiredly. "I need an answer now, miss."

Sarah smiled through happy tears as she faced John. Lately, the only thing she had wished for was the opportunity to hear John Carson tell her that he loved her and truly mean it. But now, even though he hadn't said the three words she desperately wanted to hear, she had never felt more loved by anyone.

"I'm staying!" Sarah practically shouted. She threw herself into John's arms, hugging him tightly while he twirled her around. "I'm going home."

"And will you be my wife when we get there?" John proposed.

"Now you're making my dreams come true," she whispered, refusing to let go of John, even when he returned her to the ground. "Yes, I will."

"You do realize I'll probably still say and do a lot of dumb things that will make us quarrel, don't you?"

"Of course you will, and so will I." Sarah chuckled lightly, finally pulling away enough to look up at him. "But then we can look forward to making up afterward."

"And there will be—"

"John," Sarah whispered as she rested her fingers over his mouth, "when are you going to stop talking and kiss your future wife?"

"Right after I tell her something I should have said a long time ago." He cupped her face in his hands and lowered his forehead to rest against hers. "I love you," he proclaimed, smiling as he said those special words for the first time, happy to know it wouldn't be the last.

"I love you too," Sarah murmured, happily accepting John's kiss when he pressed his lips to hers.

"Well, you two lovebirds ready to go back home?" Ned asked as he and May returned Sarah's belongings to the wagon.

"More than ever!"

Ned cautiously took Thunder's reins. "All right, then. I'll get Thunder tied up to the back of my wagon, and you and John can ride back with me and May."

"Thunder, be a good boy," Sarah told her horse when he neighed loudly. "No one's trying to take you away from me. We're all going back to Templeton, where we belong."

Taking John's hand, Sarah climbed into Ned's wagon, excited to go back to her childhood home, where she had been raised as a doctor's daughter but was returning to become a doctor's wife.